A NOVEL BY
ROBERT R. MOSS

VALOR
BOOKS

Published in the United States of America

Grateful acknowledgment is made to the following for
permission to reprint previously published material:

Hi Lo Music Inc. and the Sam Phillips Music Group for lyrics to
Rock With Me Baby by Billy Lee Riley, Jack Clement and Ronald
Wallace. Copyright © 1956 and copyright © renewed 1984 by
Hi Lo Music Inc. as well as for lyrics to *Hold Me Baby* by
James Cotton. Copyright © 1954 and copyright ©
renewed 1982 by Hi Lo Music Inc.

Shelby Singleton Music, Inc. for lyrics to *Mend Your Ways* by Leroy
Kirkland and Lincoln Chase. Copyright © 1953 and copyright ©
renewed 1981 by Shelby Singleton Music, Inc.
All rights administered by Shelby Singleton Music, Inc.

Used by permission

Publisher's Cataloging-in-Publication data
Moss, Robert R.
Descending Memphis : a novel / by Robert R. Moss.
p. cm.
ISBN 978-0-692-36422-2
1. Detective and mystery stories—Fiction. 2. Private investigators—
Tennessee—Memphis—Fiction. 3. Fathers and sons—Fiction.
4. Coming of age—Fiction. 5. Rockabilly music—Fiction.
6. Sun records—Fiction. 7. United States—Race relations—20th
century—Fiction. 8. Memphis (Tenn.)—Fiction. I. Title.
PS3613.O782 D47 2015
813.6 --dc23   2015902687

ACKNOWLEDGMENTS

There are several people I must thank. Without their help it would have been impossible for me to write this book.

Memphis historians Gene Gill and David French lived in that city during the time this story takes place and they cheerfully answered my many questions.

Ruth White's career in the Nashville music industry began in 1947 as a song plugger of sheet music at Stroebel's Music Shop. She later worked in publishing on Music Row and co-authored the life story of her husband, the renowned steel guitar player, Howard White, as well as R&B legend, Ted Jarrett. Ruth took my phone calls and provided insight into Nashville of the 1950s as two separate music cities: one white and one black.

Abdul Amin grew up outside West Memphis during the 1950s, a fact I was not to learn until some time after we met. As I approached the latter stages of writing my manuscript, I asked him to read it. Abdul graciously accepted my request and I value the candor he expressed in speaking to me about the story and what it was like to live in a segregated society.

Several other people, in addition to Abdul, read earlier drafts and I gladly thank Chris Rudolf, Dave Anolik, Jeff Marks and Ruth White for their encouragement. I also thank Ray Johnston for his generosity and advice.

I thank Jud Phillips of Hi Lo Music Inc. and the Sam Phillips Music Group, as well as John Singleton of Shelby

Singleton Music, Inc. and Sun Records for their support.

I express my appreciation to Steve Donatelli for his superb design work on the cover.

And to my wife and son, I thank you for your love and patience.

For K and T

Well, when you get started, man you don't wanna stop
It nearly drives you crazy, but your baby say rock
She said come on daddy, let's have some fun
Give everyone a laugh, and when you're dead you're done
Rock with me baby, yeah
Rock with me baby, ooh!
Rock with me baby
Don't you know your daddy wants to rock
        - Billy Lee Riley

Ah, make the most of what we yet may spend,
Before we too into the Dust descend;
Dust into Dust, and under Dust to lie
Sans Wine, sans Song, sans Singer, and—sans End
        - Omar Khayyam

1

I DREAMED about the guy who taught me guitar. Dan Turner. The colored guy my daddy used to hire to take care of the yard and stuff. Dan was singing this blues song. It has a guitar lick that sounds like a train whistle. After a while, the whistle sounded more like a bell. It was the phone. It woke me up. So I ran down the hall to get it.

"Is this Tommy Rhodeen?" asks the lady on the other end.

"Yes, who's this?"

"Claire Williams. My husband is Garland Williams."

I'm half-asleep, but I know the name. The guy's a lawyer who doesn't practice law. He's an investor. He puts his money into all sorts of things: real estate, a chain of burger joints, a trucking company; if it can make a profit, he's interested. Once he ran for mayor. He lost. I was a kid at the time, so I don't remember much about it.

"I have a job for you," she says. "Come to the house and I'll tell you about it."

I tell her I'm interested. Actually, I'm more than interested. But I don't tell her that. She gives me the address and tells me to come around ten.

I hang up the phone and go down to the kitchen. My Aunt Norma's already gone to the market, so I make my own breakfast and have a smoke. Afterward, I go up to my room. It's the room I had as a boy, but I'm the man of the house. I sit down on my bed, a twin size with a pine frame. A matching chest of drawers and a desk make up the rest of the furniture. They're solid; built to last a lifetime, the man at the store said. The desk was where I was supposed to do my homework, but rarely did. Beneath the bed I keep my guitar. It came from a pawn shop. I got it years ago; I'd saved my allowance to buy it. It's old and it goes out of tune as I play. I take my guitar out from under the bed and play that blues lick that sounds like a train whistle. That's when I remember the dream I'd told you about, the dream about the guy who taught me guitar.

Now most of my jobs are for people whose car or tools were stolen, crimes the police are unable or just too busy to solve. I find who has it, buy it back, no questions asked. But if I discover where they hid the stuff, I just take it and get it back to its rightful owner. That way I make more on my end.

One of my best jobs was finding a stolen dog. It wasn't a mutt. It was a purebred pointer that belonged to a judge. This kid cut the lock on the kennel and used a piece of meat or something. The judge loved that dog; it being stolen made him pissed. He made some calls. The cops made it their business, but they couldn't find that dog—not even so much as its bark. So when vinegar doesn't work, the judge tries honey. He posts a reward. But the kid's too scared to bring the dog back. So I pay the guy a few bucks for his trouble and return the animal. The judge wants to give me the reward. I ask if he can do me a favor instead. The judge agrees; he pushes through the paperwork for my private investigator license. That was about a year ago. The license made me legal, so to speak, but I'm still new at this and anything new takes time.

Except for the judge and a few others, most of my

customers are working people. They don't have insurance. If their stuff gets stolen, they can't afford to buy something new. Instead, they pay me to get it back. It's better than nothing. The Williamses are a whole other kind of a customer. I need something better to wear.

I put down my guitar, get up, and go down the hall to what was my daddy's bedroom. Once it had been the place of Saturday mornings spent in bed listening to stories, or where I ran to when thunder shook the house. Yeah, that was a long time ago. The knob turns, but the door is stuck. I shove my hip against it and go inside.

The room's pretty much how I remembered it. As if you could smell his tobacco and sweat and bay rum. Their wedding photo still stood on the dresser. And next to it is the velvet box that holds his medals and ribbons. I pick up the case, wipe off the dust, and open it. It gives off that tarnished brass smell. His decorations remind me of when I was little and climbed into the attic. I discovered a trunk that held a bunch of my momma's belongings, stuff my daddy saved after she had passed. I don't want to think about that. I get on with my business.

I take his gray suit out of the closet. I try it on. It looks good. The sleeves are long, but it will do. Yeah, I can call on the Williamses in that. I put on one of his ties and look in the mirror. In the reflection, I see my Aunt Norma standing near the door.

"That's fine," she says. "It's about time you made use of his clothes." She smooths the lapels, pats her big hands across my shoulders, and tugs on the sleeves.

"I'll take them in. Won't take much time. The pants look fine."

I LAY THE JACKET, now hemmed, on the backseat of my car, roll down the windows, and get going to meet the Williamses. Even with the windows down, the car heats up each time I get stuck at a light.

Soon I come to those pillars that mark the entrance to Morningside Park. I drive between them and feel like I'm a tourist in my own town. I guess you get used to it if you live or work there, but it's my first time. I drive around the bend, read the street numbers and double check the address. The Williamses live in a red brick house with six white columns. It rises up from a huge yard, the grass all mowed and without any bare spots. A brand new Cadillac sits in the driveway, so I park my old Ford at the end of the block.

I get out, put on my jacket, and walk back the way I came. I pass a colored man tending the flowers, the sun on his back; it's clear his thoughts are someplace else. My thoughts shift as I walk through the open gate to what the Williamses could be missing. In a place like this it could be anything. I continue up the driveway and on to the house. A pair of rocking chairs sits near the door. I knock. I wipe my forehead. As I stuff my handkerchief back in my pocket, I hear footsteps. The door opens.

"Can I help you, suh?" says a man with dark skin.

"Mrs. Williams called me about a job," I say.

The butler gets my name and asks if I'll wait in the foyer. The back and forth whirr of a vacuum cleaner drifts down from the second floor. It begins to whine and whoever is using it snaps it off. I look around. There's a curved staircase with a railing carved out of mahogany. To the right is a fancy living room and to the left a formal dining room. I wonder if they eat there on special occasions, or just because it's Tuesday. A clock chimes the hour, the vacuum switches on, and the butler reappears and asks me to follow. We cross the living room. The butler stops. He knocks on a door. A woman's voice says, "Come in, Samuel." He opens it and lets me pass.

"Thank you for coming, Mr. Rhodeen," says a slender woman with blonde hair. She's attractive and in her late thirties.

"I'm Claire Williams. This is my husband, Garland."

The man pushes himself up. He's huge. He walks toward me. Garland Williams appears to be nearly sixty, but despite his age and the cut of his clothes he looks more like a roustabout than a businessman. We shake hands; his are big and coarse, and his grip is strong. His body and head are large, and he has no neck. If you saw him in the dark, you'd think he's an animal. Claire Williams is his second wife and, as second wives usually are, she is lovelier than the first. The first Mrs. Williams got into car crash years ago. Neither she nor their son survived. It's the second marriage for both.

Everything in the room seems more valuable than anything I'd ever recovered, but what I notice most of all is a painting. It's of a girl. She looks about eight or nine. It isn't a formal portrait, the kind where the subject stares out of the canvas. The girl holds a cat, and they have the same green eyes, and the two appear to be looking at each other.

Mr. Williams indicates a chair and we sit down across from each other. His wife sits to his side.

"How can I help you?" I ask. "People call me when they're missing something and the police can't help. What are you missing?"

Mrs. Williams's eyes get moist and she turns them toward her husband.

"It's Helen," says Mr. Williams. "Claire's daughter from a previous marriage. She's seventeen; she's run away before, but never this long."

"How long is long?"

"It'll be one week tomorrow."

"Have you filed a report?"

Mr. Williams shakes his head.

"This is a family matter. We don't want to create any controversy and—"

"Helen enjoys making me upset," Mrs. Williams says as she gets up. "She does it to get back at me for remarrying after Stephen, my first husband, died."

"Is Helen the girl in the painting?"

Mrs. Williams walks toward it.

"Yes, that was Helen. I wish she still was."

"Where does she go to school?"

"Miss Hutchison's. Helen needs to be back before school starts."

"Do you have an idea where your daughter might be?"

Mrs. Williams comes back from the painting and sits down.

"Last time she was found in one of those awful roadhouses out in Middleton where they have those rock and roll bands. And before that, she was pulled out of another dive. That's why we thought of you."

Mrs. Williams places a hand to her mouth; her husband leans in front of her and says, "Your knowledge of that rock and roll music is why I asked Claire to call you instead of the detectives my brother suggested."

I smile. I'd made a demo at Sun Records a while back and it got played on the air a couple of times. Some people said I had talent, but not enough to make it.

"How do you know about that?" I ask.

"I make it my business to know a lot of things," Mr. Williams replies.

I nod my head.

"As far as finding Helen, I'll need a picture of her, and I'd like to speak with her friends. Can I have a list of their names?"

Mrs. Williams frowns and lights a cigarette.

"We can't have you speaking to those girls. People would talk."

"That's going to make finding Helen that much more difficult."

"You'll just have to find another way."

"Okay. Any boyfriends? Does she have a steady?"

"Helen had been seeing this older boy," Mrs. Williams says. "Dale Martins is his name. He works, of all things, at a movie theater. But she promised us she'd broken it off."

"That's good to know, but I'll check up on him all the same. Does Helen have a car?"

Mrs. Williams blows a stream of smoke at the ceiling and says, "Does she ever. Garland bought Helen a brand new Thunderbird convertible for her sixteenth birthday. She never even said a proper thank you. Helen had her eye on that car and—"

Mr. Williams clears his throat.

"Mr. Rhodeen, what do you charge for this kind of work?"

It's a question I should have prepared for, but I've never worked a case like this. I wasn't sure what to say.

"I get a percentage of what my clients pay to get back their property, but this is different."

Mr. Williams looks at me. I can tell he's waiting for me to give him a figure. I shift in my seat.

"Frankly, this is not my usual business of getting back stolen cars, tools, and television sets. But I believe I'm the right guy as far as finding your daughter."

Mr. Williams takes hold of his wife's hand. He looks into her eyes, then he turns to me.

"Would you get our Helen back for one thousand dollars?"

It's more than I expected. But before I can answer, the door opens and in walks a seventeen-year-old girl. It's over before it has started. I stand up and Mrs. Williams makes the introductions.

"June, this is Tommy Rhodeen. He's going to find Helen. Tommy, this is my niece, June, my sister's girl."

I'm still in business. June sits in the chair beside me. She's cute but seems like a priss.

"June," Garland says. "Can you tell Mr. Rhodeen anything that might help him find your cousin?"

"I've told you everything I know. She didn't like that you forbid her from going to those rock 'n' roll concerts. But she never gave me the idea she'd do anything like this."

"She never confided in you?" I ask. "Or say anything that might help us find her?"

"No, I'm afraid not."

June tells us more of what she knows about her cousin, but none of it's going to help.

Garland fidgets, then stands up and says, "All right, June. Thank you for coming."

I ask her if I can call if I have any questions, she says yes. Then June passes on a message from her momma and says goodbye. After she leaves I find myself standing between Garland and Claire.

"Do you have that picture of Helen? And a description of her car, license number and such?"

Mrs. Williams hands me a photograph. I see a girl who looks how her mother must have when she was seventeen. She has blonde hair, green eyes, and smooth skin.

"Can I see Helen's room? There could be some clues."

She leads me upstairs and opens the door. It's a girl's room. There's stuffed animals and a lot of pink. On the dresser lay magazines. There's a three-speed record player and a stack of 45s.

"Does Helen keep a diary?" I ask.

"Yes, it's how I learned about Dale, and that he... That he pressured her. You understand?"

I nod my head.

"Where does she keep it?"

"It's gone."

"Was there anything she wrote that could help us find where she went, or what she was thinking?"

"Before Dale, about six months ago, Helen wrote about a boy. It was only a few lines; she wrote he's handsome but unavailable."

"Was there a name or initials? Anything that could tell us who she meant?"

"No. She only mentioned him once."

"Did she date anyone after Dale?"

"I don't think so. At least not that I know of."

I ask if we can search the room. She gives me the okay. We go through everything: her clothes, her closet; we open her drawers and look under her bed, but find nothing that can tell us where she's gone.

The two of us return to the library. Mr. Williams is not there. In his place is a handsome man in his forties holding a briefcase.

"Oh, hello Edward," says Mrs. Williams. "Edward this

is Tommy Rhodeen, the detective we hired to find Helen. Edward is Garland's brother."

I say hello and shake his hand. Edward looks nothing like his brother. He looks like Cary Grant, only better dressed.

"Pleased to meet you, Mr. Rhodeen. I'm glad we've enlisted your help."

Garland comes back with the information about Helen's car and hands it to me. Edward turns to his brother and takes some papers out of his case.

"Garland, I need your signature before my meeting."

"Clement?"

"Some of his people."

Garland nods, glances at the documents, and signs his name. Edward gets ready to leave, and I'm ready to do the same.

"Oh, one more thing," I say. "Do you own any other property where Helen may—"

Garland lifts a hand.

"I own a cabin at Glenn Springs. I asked my chauffeur to visit it last week. No one's been there."

"Do you mind if I take a look?"

He opens a drawer, takes a key off a ring, and hands it to me.

3

THE SUN BAKES the sidewalk as I walk to my car with the envelope Mr. Williams gave me. Inside is a first installment, a check for five hundred dollars, along with the car information, a photo and a key. I light a cigarette and lean against my car in the shade. I gaze at Helen's photo. Except for her green eyes she looks nothing like the girl in the painting; she looks more like a younger version of her mother. I finish my smoke, get in the car, and drive downtown to take care of business.

"I have to ask the manager to approve this," the teller says, and she carries the check to a man at a desk. He frowns. I can't hear what they're saying. It's like they're a couple of mutes. The manager opens a long drawer, pulls out a card, and studies the two pieces of paper. He dials his phone. He speaks into it, but I still can't hear a word he says. He looks at me. His mouth stops working. He hangs up the phone and hands the check to the teller. She comes back to the window.

"What denominations would you like?" she asks.

I leave the bank with my cash, go to my car, and take off my jacket and tie. I head north. I rest my elbow out the window as I drive. I have a stop to make before I go to the cabin.

It's a quiet neighborhood where working people live in small houses, but I'm not here to see a customer. I pull up behind a Chevy and switch off the engine. Several boys play cowboys 'n' injuns in the vacant lot on the other side of the street. I get out and cross the sidewalk. The metal gate screeches. I knew it would. Jim Gantry never oils it. He wants to hear anyone coming. Dusty sheers shake in the window. As I'm about to knock, the door opens. Jim frowns and says, "Why are you here?"

I'm about to answer. My right hand is out. Jim grabs it in his left; he pulls me through the door and slams it shut with his foot. He lets go of me and turns around. An old woman sits in a recliner crocheting a blanket. I haven't seen Mrs. Gantry in ten or twelve years, and she pays us no mind as she crochets away on her balls of yarn. There are porcelain figurines and gewgaws in a curio cabinet, and none of the furniture matches.

My eyes water as the stink of cat urine wafts by. I use the back of my hand to wipe away the sting. I blink and see Jim dangling a long .44 in his hand before he sticks it under a sofa cushion.

"Haven't I told you? Never come here."

"I thought you wouldn't mind. I brought what I owe."

Jim licks his lips and says, "All of it?"

I nod. A fly buzzes about my face. I shoo it away. I pull out the wad of bills. Jim steps forward as I count.

"Twenty, forty, sixty, eighty. One hundred. Twenty, forty, sixty, eighty. Two hundred. Twenty, forty, sixty, eighty. Three hundred."

I hand Jim the cash. He puts it into the wallet he has chained to his belt. For a moment I think he smiles. "You want anything?" he asks.

"No, I'm good, thanks."

"On the house."

I shake my head. He shrugs his shoulders.

"Suit yourself."

I nod back and tell him about the new job. Jim tries not to show it, but he looks impressed. He goes in the kitchen, takes the percolator off the stove, and brings it to the sofa with another cup. We sit. He pours me a coffee and refills his own, lights a cigarette and says, "Hey, you seen Bob Oakley?"

"No, has he got out?"

"Last month. Came out with more scars than when he went in. He won't be getting into trouble in Arkansas anytime soon."

"I never did visit him," I say. "Did you?"

Bob picks up a flyswatter and uses it.

"Once. Enough to know I'd never want to end up there."

We drink our coffee, and Jim relays me stories Bob told him about doing time at Cummins State Farm. He tells me what he knows of the long line riders; the men, armed with rifles, on horseback, who oversaw the prisoners chopping and picking cotton. Bob had told him about the strap and this thing called *the Tucker Telephone*. According to Bob, the prisoners worked ten-hour days, six days a week in fields so muddy they'd drill holes in their spades to let out the water.

Jim finishes his story. Neither of us speaks. I turn the chipped cup in my hand and take a sip. One of the cats skulks along the edge of the sofa. It tries to rub up against my leg. I jostle my foot.

Then Jim crushes out his cigarette and says, "When you was a kid, you have any idea how we'd all turn out?"

I look down at the floor.

"Well at the time, I never gave it much thought."

"Me neither," he says.

I set my cup down and ask, "Was there something back then you wanted to be?"

Jim smiles and finishes his coffee.

"Yeah, a cowboy. Go out west where there weren't so

many people."

"Why didn't you?"

"Turns out I got a fear of horses."

Jim laughs. His mother looks up and asks what's so funny. We just shake our heads and laugh some more. But the laughter is there to cover what both of us are thinking. Neither of us has ever talked about fear. It's something we didn't do. We look at each other, each knowing what's in the other's head.

After that I get up. I say so long and leave. I watch the boys play across the street as I walk to my car. Their whoops and hollers merge with sound of Webb Pierce singing on the radio from the house next door.

I get back on the road to check out Garland's cabin. I've known Jim Gantry and Bob Oakley since we were kids. Of the three of us, I'm the only one who never did spend a night in jail. Jim's two years older than me and the youngest of five children. Now he's an amphetamine dealer and a sometimes money-lender, who occasionally tips me off as to who might have something I've been hired to find. Bob, I haven't seen since before I got drafted. The three of us were once like those boys I saw playing across the street.

4

THE OPEN WINDOWS cool me down on the ride. I follow the directions. I get onto a dirt road and make a left at the fork. The forest is dark and primitive. You'd expect to find a split log cabin with a mudsill floor, but what I find is built within the past ten years. It may be just a few rooms and a porch, but it's the perfect place for a hideout if you'd just robbed a bank or something and needed to a place to lay low.

I park in front. Bits of light glint through the leaves where the cove of a lake extends like a crooked finger behind the cabin. I take my flashlight from under the seat as I get out. I look down. I see tire tracks from three cars in the dirt. I crouch down. Only one set appears fresh. The other two would have been there last week. Mr. Williams's chauffeur would have seen them. I rise and look at the cabin. I hear the wind blow off the lake and through the leaves. I sense the wind on my face. The air feels cool. It's a nice place. It's good to be able to have nice places. I look up and see a hawk glide above the trees.

I walk away from the tire tracks and to the cabin. It's faced with hickory. A stone chimney juts from the roof, which is covered with shake shingles. It doesn't look like anyone's home. I could have unlocked the door and gone inside, but before I do I want to see it from all sides. I want to know if there's another door. I'd once lost getting back a stolen TV because I didn't first check out the place. Since then I've been more careful. I walk around the cabin. The windows are closed, the curtains are drawn, and there's no back door. It looks empty, but you never know. As I come back around, I step onto the porch. I knock. No one answers. I unlock the door.

I scan the place with my flashlight. There's a wooden table and above it hangs a lantern. The table has a pair of chairs. A can of beer sits at each end. I tap one with the end of my flashlight. It sounds empty. I light the lantern and adjust its wick. A wash of light illuminates the room. Photographs from hunting trips emerge on a wall, and among them is a framed quotation. I walk over to read it.

"And to every beast of the earth, and to every fowl of the air, and to every thing that creepeth upon the earth, wherein there is life, I have given every green herb for meat, and it was so."

It's from the Book of Genesis. I look closer at the photos. They're all of Garland standing next to animals he's killed. He seems at least ten or more years younger in the pictures, some as much as twenty. In one he stands next to an enormous bear while cradling a bolt-action rifle. The animal's chin has crushed the torn grass around it. Its paws spread forward as if it's asleep, yet its small eyes stare into the camera. The inscription reads: 'Grizzly Male, Shoshone National Forest, Wyoming, 1938."

I look around the rest of the room. There's a stack of movie magazines on a coffee table. The one on top is recent. The table stands in front of a couch that faces the fireplace. On the table, beside the magazines, is an ashtray and inside are cigarette butts. Some have traces of lipstick, some do not.

There's at least two more rooms to go through. I place my ear against the doors. I open one and look inside. The room contains a bare mattress on a narrow bed and a chest of drawers. My shoes make prints in the dust. I close the door and try the other room. There's a large bed. The sheets are unmade. I open the curtains to let in the light. Two cigarette butts are in the ashtray on the nightstand. I look under the bed. Something's there. I reach in with my shoe and drag out a pair of girl's pink underpants. I kick them back under the bed.

I go outside, lock the door, and walk past the three sets of tire tracks. Either Mr. Williams's chauffeur didn't tell him everything he saw, or someone came after he left. Either way, someone's been here. I need to know who.

5

I WENT TO THE MOVIES after dinner, not because I want to see Jimmy Stewart and Doris Day romp around the screen. The guy Helen had been seeing, this Dale Martins, is the assistant manager at the Malco and he's working the night shift. It had rained earlier and the neon reflects off the pavement in front of the theater. I buy a ticket, go inside, and get a bag of popcorn. The movie's underway; an usherette guides me to a seat. I watch for several minutes before I get up to find her.

"There's something wrong with the sound," I say.

The usherette scowls and says, "It sounds fine to me."

"Not to me."

"Do you want a refund?"

"I want to speak with the manager."

She sighs and we walk to the lobby.

"Wait here," she says as she climbs the stairs. I go get an Orange Crush at the stand.

She comes back with the projectionist. A creepy guy with skin the color of boiled cabbage, and beside him stands Dale Martins. I know it's him because his name is stitched on his blazer. Mrs. Williams had referred to him an *older boy.* So I expected him to be just a few years older than Helen, but he looks a year or two older than me.

"What seems to be the trouble?" Dale asks.

"Something's wrong with the sound."

"I'm sorry. Would you like a refund?"

"No, I want you to fix it."

Dale crosses his arms and says, "We can't do anything while the picture's running."

I get my money back and leave the theater as it begins to rain. I go into a place around the corner and get a bowl of chili. A cockroach scuttles from behind a napkin dispenser. I crush it with a piece of newspaper and drop it on the floor. No one notices. After I eat, I smoke a cigarette and drink coffee till it's ten minutes before the last show ends. I pay and run back to my car in the rain.

Thunder rattles the car as I park near the corner across from the theater. It's a perfect spot; I can keep a lookout on the main and side exits. Rain rolls down the windshield projecting pink and green neon-colored veins along the dashboard. The main doors open and the audience runs into the storm. They run bunched up in pairs and in fours, as if they are a herd of cattle at a river crossing. They look skittish at the water flowing through the gutter before they jump across.

I wipe the glass, have another smoke, and watch. Soon they turn off the marquee and several employees leave the side doors. Dale isn't among them.

Five more minutes pass and the side doors open. It's a man and he runs in the rain toward the parking lot. I recognize him as the projectionist. An old Dodge coupe skids to a stop by the side door a minute later. The projectionist jumps out and unlocks the trunk. The exhaust eddies around his ankles.

The side doors open again. Dale maneuvers a big box, like a seaman's chest, on a dolly to the curb. The two struggle to lift it into the back of the car. They get it in and slam the trunk shut. Dale races to the driver's seat. The projectionist climbs in on the other side.

Dale puts the car into gear and heads east on Beale. I follow. The wheels of my car part the water as the wipers sway back and forth. Neon signs twist and roll along the car hoods. Their reflections stretch like the ones you see in the mirrors at a carnival. He drives two blocks, turns on Third, I do the same. There's little traffic; it looks like an easy tail-job. A truck pulls away from the curb and cuts me off. It's only for a few seconds, but enough for me to lose sight of Dale. I gun the engine, pass the truck, and squint through my rain-smeared windshield. The Dodge reappears. I get behind him. He isn't getting away.

The next several blocks are a straight shot. I ease off to give him distance. I don't want Dale to get wise. He rounds the corner. I stomp on the brakes. A man steps in front of my car, his head under an umbrella. I honk. He runs. I give it the gas and turn the corner. The Dodge is gone. Where?

I peep right and left at the next intersection. Dale's heading north and about to make a left. I catch up just as he stops in front of a big brick building. I pull my car against the curb and douse the lights. A man in a raincoat looms from the shadows. He climbs into the back of the Dodge. Dale makes a U-turn. I duck down as his car slithers past. I jockey around and see him make a right. He turns again onto Poplar and now I'm close behind. Dale parks and kills the engine. They jump out of the car, their slicker collars turned up to the rain, and run into a building. The ground floor houses a radio repair shop. Apartments fill the level above. A light flashes on in one. I park across the street.

Lightning cracks, but the rain has stopped. The road stands empty. I keep a set of picks for repo work. I take a pair out of my kit and get my flashlight. I drop the light in my pocket as I get out of the car. I palm the tools against my leg and cross the street. I stop behind Dale's car to tie my shoe. I look up over my shoulder to make sure the lights in the apartment are on. I insert the picks into the lock. I give them a twist, the trunk pops open. I snap on my flashlight and look inside. Two brass clasps hold the chest shut. I peek over my shoulder. The light in the apartment is out. I throw open the lid. Inside the chest are six octagonal metal boxes, the kind used to hold reels of motion picture film. I close everything and hurry back to my car as a light mist begins to fall.

6

I WAKE UP EARLY. I made a mistake. I should have taken the girl's underpants at the cabin. I should have asked Mrs. Williams if they belonged to Helen. I have to go back.

Once off the highway, the road is filled with mud and puddles. I slow down. I come to the fork. I take the one on the right. I'll sneak back to the cabin instead of pulling up in my car. The road widens ahead and there's enough room to turn the car around. I switch off the motor and listen. All I hear is a few birds. A squirrel barks from a branch that arcs overhead. I get out. The sun shines above the treetops, but it is dim below, and the wind blows drops of rainwater off the leaves and branches.

I stay to the side of the road, up on the edge, and out of sight of anyone who could be coming or going. As I round the bend, I peer from behind a tree. There's no cars in front of the cabin. I walk toward it. The road's muddy and I catch myself before I slip. All of the tire tracks lay under a puddle. A woodpecker works above me in the trees. The curtains are drawn. I step onto the porch. A board creaks. I freeze. I wait in case anyone's heard. I take another step. I knock. No one answers. I unlock the door.

"Hello?" I call out.

There's no reply. I turn on my flashlight. I look at the table. The beer cans are gone. I check out the bedroom. No girl's underpants lay under the bed. No cigarette butts fill the ashtrays. Everything's been wiped fresh. A second pair of shoe prints has smeared the dust in the other bedroom. I'm too late. Any clues are gone. I go back out the way I came. As I drive, I think about going to see Mr. Williams. I could tell him what I saw at the cabin, but then he'd know I messed up.

*   *   *

That evening I go back to the movies. At the ticket booth, I ask for Dale. People buy tickets, more get in line, I stand to the side. Dale comes through the back of the booth, exchanges spots with the attendant, and takes a look through the glass.

"You!" he says. "You're the joker who complained about the sound!"

I nod.

"That's not why I'm here."

"Then what's this about?"

I indicate the people with my eyes and say, "We should talk in private."

"What are you talking about?" Dale asks.

"I'm talking about six reels of motion picture film leaving the theater last night."

His face turns white.

"Let's go to my office."

Dale opens the door to let me inside. The air conditioning rushes past me and over the sidewalk. We walk across the lobby, climb the staircase, and turn a corner. He opens a door. The walls of his office are covered with movie posters and one-sheets. We aren't alone. A redhead smokes a cigarette on a couch crammed against the wall. She looks about twenty and wears a pink top and a black skirt.

"Scram, Peggy," he says while keeping his eyes on me.

The redhead takes another drag before she realizes Dale's talking to her.

"What?" she says, as if the word has an extra syllable.

Dale frowns as he runs his hand through his hair.

"You heard me. Beat it, Peggy. I got business."

"But, Dale, you promised."

"Shut it. Take a walk."

The redhead crushes out her cigarette, hoists herself up, and leaves. Dale slams the door shut. He locks it. He mutters something, shakes his head, and takes a seat at his desk before he lights a cigarette.

"Okay, smart guy, what's this about?" he asks as he waves out the match.

I sit in the chair diagonally across from him. I'm not a hundred percent sure what I'm going to say, but I just let it spill. I sound like one of the guys in the B-movies they show.

"Nice little racket you got. So some rich guy gets a yen for a certain movie actress and needs to have her in his collection. He's got to watch her all alone in his private theater. No one to disturb him."

Dale gulps and eyeballs a drawer in his desk while I continue describing his operation.

"So you fake the paperwork to look like the inventory went back to the distributor. Only it didn't. And you take home an extra payday courtesy of Hollywood, U.S.A."

Dale grits his teeth and looks at the drawer.

"I got a cousin in Nashville who manages a theater," I say. "They got the same racket."

"Who are you?"

"Just a guy."

He keeps sneaking peeks at the drawer. I don't like it.

"I'm not looking for another business partner," Dale

says.

His hand inches forward. I come down on it with the ashtray from on top of the desk. He grabs his hand as I whip open the drawer and pull out a pistol. I yank back the slide and point the gun at his belly.

"That's some cannon you got here," I say.

"I think you broke my hand," Dale whines. He cradles it in his left and looks at me as if I'm the bully.

"It ain't broken. Besides, you're the one who went for the gun."

There's a knock. I gesture. Dale plays it cool. Only whoever it is doesn't get the message, and the knocking gets louder and faster.

"Go away! Can't you see I'm busy!" Dale shouts.

The knocking stops.

I shuck out a cigarette and light it.

"I'm not trying to muscle in," I tell him. "I got other interests."

Dale rubs his hand. It hurts more now than when I hit it.

"What other interests?" he asks.

"Helen Williams."

"Helen? What about her?"

"You still seeing her?"

Dale sneers and says, "You must be kidding. Who gave you that idea? I stopped going with that girl months ago."

"That's not what I heard."

"What?"

"I heard she broke it off."

Dale laughs, then winces at his hand.

"That screwy chick? Nothing but a tease. Doesn't put out. All talk. I kicked her to the curb."

"When's the last time you saw her?"

"Two months ago. I haven't seen her since. I gotta go get some ice."

"Okay."

I flip up the safety and lower the hammer.

"I need to keep this," I say.

Dale nods his head as I back out the door. I close it and walk away. I keep myself from laughing as I take the stairs. I got a cousin in Nashville, but he doesn't work at a theater. I made a lucky guess, but I'm nowhere closer to finding Helen.

7

A RABBIT RUNS across the road and the man driving the Cadillac Eldorado swerves to meet it. Motoring along a two-lane road that cuts through a marshy forest, the driver takes advantage of the V8 engine's 305 horsepower as well as the factory-installed air conditioning.

With one hand on the steering wheel, he uses the other to turn up the volume on the radio. There's no one in the back, so the driver has tuned in to ten-seventy on the AM dial. It isn't a station his employer would listen to.

The deejay begins an outrageous radio patter full of rhyming and signifying and speaking to the astounding benefits of a particular brand of pomade. The assertions go miles beyond what can be achieved through even the most exaggerated claims related to anything tonsorial. Then he hollers out the time and the station's call letters before playing *Hold Me Baby* by James Cotton.

The man enjoys these times when he drives with no one in the back, which means he can listen to Nat D. Williams, or Rufus Thomas, or some of the other colored announcers on the radio. Furthermore, the Cadillac serves as an extension of himself and it seems to make up for things he cannot control, such as his height.

And right now, even though he is only running an errand for his employer, he can pretend that he owns such a fine and fancy automobile. In fact, in a year or two, he plans to own a similar car. Except his is going to be a convertible in cherry red. He turns the radio louder.

He taps his hand on the wheel as he sings along with James Cotton.

> "Hold me baby
> Hold me in your arms
> Hold me baby
> Hold me in your arms
> You can squeeze and love me
> Baby, all night long.

> "Say she's mean?
> Treats me nice and kind
> Say she's mean?
> Treats me nice and kind
> Don't worry about my baby
> Because I know she's mine all the time."

But he stops singing when he notices a brand new two-tone, blue and white Mercury Montclair parked on the side of the road. He also notices the hood is up. And what's more, he notices a high yellow woman with a complexion like a tan paper bag standing and waving beside the car. She wears a tight red dress that reveals a pair of well-formed legs. She has fine features, and she wears her hair cut short with curls like Dorothy Dandridge. And being a man, he pulls over to get a better view. She looks drop-dead gorgeous and she looks like she needs help.

The man brings the Cadillac to a stop. He steps out of the car and into the steamy air, oversweet with honeysuckle, and shuts the door with a whack. He's five-foot-four with two-inch lifts in his shoes and he's conscious of his small strides as he walks the twenty yards back down the road. To make up for his lack of height, the man affects a rolling swagger.

"Can't git her started?" he asks.

"No. It was driving fine. Then there was this noise and the car died. So I pulled over. My man's gonna kill me when he hears about this. Oh, he told me to never mess with his car."

The man beams as he says, "Aw, he don't need to know nothin'. Lemme take a look."

She smiles back and says, "Would you?"

"Sure I will. I know me a thing about cars."

The man removes his chauffeur's jacket, as if he is a surgeon preparing for an operation, and he holds it out to her. She takes it and folds it with care while the man rolls up his sleeves.

"Sugar, try to start her while I listen to the engine."

He opens the car door for her and watches her legs as she slides onto the seat. She twists the key. The car goes chugga chugga chugga chugga.

"Try again, sweetheart."

She does and the car keeps making the same chugga chugga. That's when another man, a big colored man, steps from behind the trees. He has a body and face like a bear. His eyes seem too small for his head. He creeps toward the guy leaning over the engine.

"One more time," he tells her.

The car goes chugga chugga chugga chugga. And the noise covers the last two footsteps, the swish of the tire iron, and the grunt as the man crumples to the ground. Then the motor catches, the engine starts. The assailant scoops up the man and swings him into the trunk. He tosses in the tire iron, slams the trunk shut, and slides through the open door and onto the passenger seat. The woman leans over and kisses him on the mouth as they speed down the empty road.

8

THAT NIGHT I DROVE to Middleton. I went to the Hideaway, the roadhouse where they found Helen the last time she ran away from home. I pass by fields and farms and a few houses until the highway turns into Main Street. I drive past a feed store and a barbershop, a mechanic's and a filling station. I cross the railroad tracks and I soon come upon a low, nondescript building.

The sign promises *Cold Beer*. The Hideaway is true to its name. I park in the gravel lot and walk past the cars. I step inside and take in the scene. Lloyd McCollough and his band are on stage.

I walk through the crowd to the bar. A hand taps me on the shoulder. I turn and get an uppercut to the chin. I nearly fall backward—more from the surprise than anything else—but I'm ready to return the punch. Two gorillas grab my arms.

"That's payback, Rhodeen!"

A punk in a pair of dungarees and a western shirt is making his fists. They rotate like they're peddling a bike. It's the first time I've seen him. I don't know who he is or his name. I break my arms free. His friends replace their hands loosely on my shoulders. I taste rust in my mouth and swallow the blood.

"Payback for what?" I say.

"That brand new Coupe deVille. I'd swiped it and you came along and took it before I fenced it."

I laugh. His eyes pop out of his head.

"You thought you could hide a Cadillac under a tarp on the street? Boy, you need to do better than that."

The punk takes a step toward me. He's just inches from my face.

"Well, you owe me," he says. "You owe me a finder's fee."

I keep laughing.

"How you figure that?"

His mouth tries to form the words that his brain can't conceive, and his cheeks turn hamburger-pink. Then he stammers out, "Possession is some percent of the law."

I guffaw even more.

"That ain't the expression," I tell him. "It's 'possession is nine-tenths of the law.' And here's how it works. I took possession of that Cadillac Coupe deVille because you did such a lousy job hiding it. All I had to do was find it and use the spare key the owner lent me. So I don't owe you nothing."

People start laughing. The punk slips through the crowd. His sidekicks look at each other. One shrugs his shoulders, they leave. Everyone else goes back to watching the band, or dancing, or drinking, and I walk to the bar. I wave at Paul. He's working the other end. He waves back, opens a bottle of beer for a guy, and comes over.

"Hey, Tommy. Friend of yours?"

"Oh, yeah, we go way back."

"Thirsty?"

"Yeah, a beer would be all right."

Paul pops the top off a bottle. I take a swig.

"Haven't seen you in a while," he says. What've you been up to? You still doing the recovery thing?"

I nod my head and say, "Yeah, but I'm branching out into new territory."

I set Helen's photo on the bar.

"You seen her? Name's Helen Williams. Used to come around here a while back."

Paul picks up the photo and grins.

"Sure, I know her. That gal's got a mouth on her, Helen has. She could teach a sailor how to curse. But she hasn't been back since she got dragged out. That was what? Three months ago?"

"Thanks, Paul. I had a feeling she's changed her hangout. But it's good to see you."

I turn my head to the tables and say, "This Helen have any friends here? Anyone who might know where she is?"

Paul scans the room and points to two brunettes.

"Yeah. Barbara and Ruth. Try them. Barbara's the one facing our way."

The two have their hair in pony-tails. They're good looking, but in an easy way. Helen would have been the standout. I walk over.

"Hi Barbara. And you must be Ruth. Hi."

They look up at me and then at each other.

"Do we know you?" Ruth asks.

"No. My name's Tommy. Mind if I sit down?"

"It's a free country," says Barbara. "Especially if you buy us a drink."

I catch the waitress's attention. After she takes their order, I pull out the photo and set it on the table.

"Know her?"

Ruth picks it up, takes a quick glance, and hands it to her friend. Barbara looks at it and puts it face down on the table.

"Yeah, we know her," says Ruth.

"Know where I can find her?"

Barbara makes a face and a sound that isn't too ladylike.

"Why on Earth are you looking for her?"

"Her family hired me to."

Barbara sniggers and slaps her hand on the table.

"That bitch hasn't been here since she got reeled in."

"And it's not like she left a forwarding address," Ruth adds.

"Which guys was she keeping company with? Anyone you can point to?"

The girls break into hysterics. The waitress comes back with their drinks. The two try to lose their giggles.

Ruth gestures with the photo and says, "This girl tried to get every good lookin' guy to make a play for her. She made each one think he had a chance and then she left them in the dust." Ruth tosses the photo at me.

"Men!" declares Barbara, and the two start laughing again.

"Was she interested in any of the guys in the bands?"

Ruth stops laughing.

"Well, I suppose but she wasn't too particular about the music. She just likes whatever's popular."

I thank them, which makes them laugh even harder. I get up and go back to the bar.

"Any luck?" Paul asks.

I shake my head as I tell him, "Not even a teensy bit. Seems Helen sure made herself well-liked around here."

Paul chuckles as he wipes the bar.

"I thought you'd get something like that."

I point my bottle to the band on stage.

"Glad Lloyd gave up the hillbilly thing. He's got a good voice for rock 'n' roll."

Paul nods and gets a beer for another guy.

I take a drink and watch the cigarette smoke float up into the lamplight. I can't imagine the girl in the painting with Barbara and Ruth. I show the photo to other people at the bar. No one knows where she is.

I watch Lloyd and his band finish their set. I say goodbye to Paul as a band I don't like gets up on stage. I go over to Lloyd and his guys. I ask them if they know Helen and if they've seen her lately. They groan at the mention of her name. They all agree things are better without her; they've no idea where she's gone.

The other band begins to play, and I go outside. I hear footsteps behind me. I turn around and see the punk.

"You still owe me a finder's fee," he says.

"You're a broken record, kid."

He pulls a knife and pushes the button. The narrow blade flips open and catches the light.

"Nothing doing. You're not gonna chisel me."

He takes a step in my direction.

"Where's your two gorillas, your goons?" I say. "Isn't that how you operate?"

The punk cackles in a singsong voice, "Just you and me and my blade makes three."

I roll my eyes.

"Come on, cut the tough-guy act. You've been watching too many movies."

He coughs up a lunger and spits it at me. It lands with a splat between us, but I'm not laughing.

"I'm going to ask you nicely, put away the knife and go home."

He doesn't reply. We circle each other. He feints with the knife. I use my hands. The punk springs forward; I dodge to my left; the blade punctures the side of my shirt.

We circle once more. His eyes stare into mine. Sweat drips off his chin. He lunges at me. This time I'm ready. I step to my left and grab his forearm with both hands. I crank it against my hip. Then I give him a right hook to his nose. The cartilage snaps. He yelps and lets go of the knife. It clatters to the ground. I step on the blade with my heel.

Before he knows what I'm doing, I reach down and grab hold of it. I yank up on the handle so the blade snaps off beneath my boot. In a single move, I drop the broken handle and rotate up with my right into his belly. I follow with a left across his already broken nose.

I hear a gasp. A couple going to their car does a double take. They rush back inside the bar. I grab the punk by his shirt collar and toss him onto the hood of my car. I lean into his pimply face.

"You still want your finder's fee!" I shout.

The kid groans. I wipe my car with him with like a dirty rag. I push him down to the gravel. He curls up in a ball, expecting to feel my boot in his kidneys.

My hands are streaked with the punk's blood. My shirt is also marked. I'm too revolted to take it further. I wipe my forehead with the back of my hand. I light up a smoke and flick the match at the punk on the ground.

I get in my car and speed off, kicking up a load of gravel. My body shakes, my heart beats fast, and my lungs can't get enough air. I toss the cigarette out the window. A shower of sparks explodes into the night.

9

I HAVE A HUNCH. The Williamses haven't reported Helen's car as stolen. She'll need cash to be away this long. I start that morning at the larger dealers on Union. No one's seen that Thunderbird, so I try the smaller lots.

Trip's Used Cars is the fourth. The cars look clean and there's a red Thunderbird that matches the description. I walk up to get a better look.

"Thunderbird. Nice car, but that old coupe of yours... What is that a '46? I can't give you much on a trade."

I turn around and see a man in his forties. His face and neck are tan. He has on a sport coat and a porkpie hat. His hands are stuffed in his pockets; he rattles the change.

"Not looking to buy," I say. "But I am searching for a car like that? Mind if I check the VIN?"

The man frowns and says, "It ain't stolen."

"I didn't say it is. I'm looking for the owner."

He goes back to rattling his change.

"Who are you?"

I show him my P.I. license and give him my name.

He settles down, but his eyes remain wary. He lifts his hat and rubs a hand through his hair.

"What VIN you looking for?"

I open the paper. A drop of sweat falls onto the ink. "P5FH148201."

"It's unlocked, I'll pop the hood."

We look at the plate.

"Satisfied?"

I nod my head. He slams the hood shut.

"Yeah, thank you," I say. "I didn't mean to rile you."

"No hard feelings. My name's Trip Rudder."

We shake hands and he tells me I can write down the VIN, and that he'll let me know if the car comes in.

As we walk to his office he says, "That old Ford of yours has seen better days. Can I show you something?"

I shake my head no and say, "I got it second hand. It runs a whole better than it looks."

As we walk a customer steps onto the lot. Trip waves to him, turns to me and says, "Go inside. Give Evelyn your number."

The small building at the back of the lot is cinderblock and has a metal roof. There's not much inside, a desk and some chairs. A door leads to a backroom.

"Hello?" I call out.

The door opens, a girl steps through. She's pretty, about twenty years old. She smiles. She doesn't seem stuck up. She has brown hair and eyes. She wears make-up, but not too much.

"Are you Evelyn?"

"Yes."

"Trip said you could help me."

"He did, did he?"

"Yeah, I'm trying to track down a '55 Thunderbird. Trip said I could leave the VIN and my phone number with you."

Evelyn holds out a pad of paper and a pen. I take them and write down the information, along with my name and number. I tear it off and hand it to her.

"What's your number?" I ask with pen on paper.

"What for?"

"To ask you out for Friday night."

"What's stopping you now?"

"Nothing. Let's you and me go out."
"Sorry, I have a date. But I'm free Thursday."
I shake my head and laugh. Evelyn laughs, too.
"Okay, Thursday. What's your address?"
"Just pick me up here at six."
"All right, I will. My name's Tommy."
She holds up the paper and says, "I know."

10

THE NEXT MORNING, I eat breakfast, go up to my room, and tune my guitar. I play a few songs. I try to write one. It isn't coming so I work out the chords to a Johnnie Burnette song. Then I go back to mine. I don't get far. The phone rings. Aunt Norma picks it up. It's for me. The guy sounds like he's calling from a phone booth. He describes a thing I was hired a week ago for. He tells me to be at a spot near the river at noon. I hang up and go back to my guitar.

A lot of these recovery jobs take time. It takes a while for word to get out and for the thief to call me back. Usually, five or six days. Sometimes more. That's why it's best to have a bunch of these jobs going on at the same time.

Anyhow, it's time to go. I get in my car, but pull over after only a couple of blocks. Reflecting in the sunlight is a pickaxe striking the ground beside a tree stump. It's hefted by a strong colored man. He wears his hair shaved close and his neck muscles show above his wide shoulders. His clothes are stained with sweat and dirt. I watch him work on that stump and, in my mind, I go back fifteen or more years to my own backyard.

"Hey, Dan, what are you doing?"

"Getting rid of this here, tree stump."

"How come?"

"Well, this ol' tree took ill."

"It's sick?"

"Uh-huh."

"There's nothing you can do for it?"

"No. There ain't no cure. This tree got somethin' that spreads. Like the flu, and it pass on to the others. Make 'em sick. Kill 'em too."

"So you had to cut it down?"

"Yeah, your daddy said cut it down. And now I gots to get it out, roots and all."

"It hard?"

"Sure it's hard. What tree wants to leave this here, Earth?"

"So how you gonna do it?"

"Chopping down this tree? That was the easy part. Then I hads to gather it all up and haul it away. Now I gotta dig out the roots."

"How you gonna do that?"

"That's the hard part. I gonna use this pickaxe, saw and shovel. Dig all around them roots. Cut 'em out best I can."

"That it?"

"No, that ain't it. I gots to build a fire and keep it burning. Burning until what's left of these ol' roots ain't nothing more but ash."

"Then it's gone?"

"Then it's gone."

I look out the window and watch the man attack the ground with the pickaxe. Sweat rolls down his face. His arms and muscles are like how I remember Dan's. Dan would be in his sixties by now, and I have no idea where he's gone. I asked around some years ago, but Dan is as gone as those tree roots.

The car has heated up, parked there on the street like it was. I wipe off my forehead and restart the car. The man chops at the stump. He'll be at it all day, maybe even the next. I drive on to meet the guy who called.

I get there early and take a look around. A barge with a shipment of Chevrolets is tied up along the edge of the river. It's not far from where the guy wants to meet. I watch fellas my age offload the cars. They drive them down the ramp, over the cobblestones, and on to a lot somewhere. They're all in a hurry. It's a good place to do a deal; no one there has time to bother with me. I lean against my car. The sun feels good on my face. A tug pushes a barge up river and gulls fly overhead and I listen to the sounds of the waterfront.

At noon, a cream-colored milk truck with red fenders rolls by. It parks in front of me. I wait a minute and then walk past the truck. A man inside pretends to read the paper. He needs a shave. I figure he's the guy. I turn around, walk back, and knock on the door of the truck.

"You call me?"

He coughs and says, "Might could."

"Look, I got work to do. Did you call me or not?"

He puts down the paper and says, "Sure, I called you. I got it here in my truck."

"Let me in."

He coughs again, gets up, and opens the door. I climb in and say, "Okay, let's see it."

He shakes his head and says, "Show me the money."

I fan the bills for him to see. He hands me a paper bag he got from behind his seat. I look inside. There's something wrapped in newspaper. I take it out and open it.

"That's it, right?" he asks.

"Yeah, that's it."

It's silver, some kind of pointer stolen from a Jewish temple.

"Why'd you take only this?" I ask. "There was plenty stuff more valuable."

"It wasn't me. It was my nephew. He went in on a dare. Broke a window. The kid didn't know what to do. So he come out with that. Who's gonna want that thing? It's scarcely worth the trouble to melt down. I heard you was going around asking about it, so I made the call."

I nod my head and give him the cash. I put the silver thing in the bag. I get out of the truck and get back in my car. I hear the milk truck start up and drive away.

The pointer was stolen from a Jewish temple downtown. The rabbi got my name from a man who owns a pawn shop. I'd never met a rabbi before. He asked me to come to his office. He wasn't like what I expected. Rabbi Waxman told me his granddaddy came to Memphis from Europe when he was a kid and fought for the Confederacy. Imagine that. But he seems like a straight up guy. And that's important in my line of work. There's no contracts. No pieces of paper. Everything's on a handshake and a nod and, even for a Jew, the rabbi seems like someone I can trust. In fact, maybe more so than most of the people I do business with.

I start my car and get going to bring the rabbi his pointer. I take Union over to Third and up to Poplar, and find a spot to park. I stand in front of the massive building. A pair of spires rises into the air. Set between them is a stained glass window forming a Star of David. I walk up the stairs, through an arch, and open the door.

Inside the air is cool. You can't hear the noise from the street. An old colored man pushes a mop on the tiles. I ask him where I can find the rabbi. He says to look in his office. I know the way.

Rabbi Waxman's on the phone, but he nods for me to come in and sit down. Above his head hangs a framed reproduction of Abraham and Isaac on Mount Moriah. The rabbi finishes his call and says, "My son, he's at

Vanderbilt studying medicine."

The rabbi points to the bag on my lap.

"Looks like you had good hunting."

I place the bag on his desk. He opens it and peers inside. He unwraps the paper and smiles as he holds the silver rod. It has a hand pointing its finger on the end of it. The rabbi nods and unlocks his desk. He takes out a cashbox and pays me the amount we agreed on.

"Thank you, Tommy. I thought we'd never get this back."

He offers me a cigarette and asks how I am. I tell him I have a job with a family on Morningside Place. He looks impressed. We then gab a bit about Sid Bernstein, one of his members, who's the fella that gave him my name. We shake hands and I leave.

Back in the car, I look at the money. It isn't near as much as I'll get when I find Helen. Still, it might be enough for a down payment. I drive over to Frank's Music. He has a Gibson I tried a couple of times and I need a new guitar.

"Hey, Frank," I say as I open the door.

Frank looks up from restringing a Martin.

"Hey, Tommy."

I look up at the spot on the wall. The Gibson isn't there. A Telecaster hangs in its place.

"Where's the ES one-twenty-five?"

"Sold it Tuesday."

"That's too bad."

Frank stops restringing the guitar. He looks at me and says, "Oh, you were gonna buy it, were you?"

"Well soon. I'm working on a big job."

"Really?"

"Yeah. And not my usual small potato stuff, either."

"You serious?"

"Would I be wasting your time if I wasn't?"

He laughs and says, "That's all you've ever done."

I put my hand to my chest and pretend I got shot in the heart and say, "Come on, Frank, why you got to say a thing like that?"

He picks up a pliers and puts it in the drawer.

"You still playing that old pawn shop guitar?"

I roll my eyes.

Frank shakes his head and says, "Why do I bother?" He slides the curtain, goes in back, and comes out with a beautiful guitar. "A Gretsch," Frank says. "A 6120 Chet Atkins with a Bigsby tailpiece." He hands it to me. The guitar feels as great as it looks. I take a pick from a dish on the counter and pluck each string one at a time.

"Can I plug her in?" I ask.

"Sure, use that Fender Champ."

I check the tuning, strum some chords, and turn up the volume before launching into *Tear It Up*. The tone is bright; it's got a growl underneath. It's the sound I want.

Frank smiles and crosses his arms.

"You best not be wasting my time."

I shake my head no as a grin slides across my face, and I play another song.

"Come back with the money," he says as I hand him the guitar.

"Frank, I'd like to talk with you about that."

*   *   *

I leave the store. Frank doesn't go for my down payment idea; he says it's policy or something like that, nothing personal. I walk back to my car thinking how finding a missing girl is not like finding a stolen box of tools. I'm in over my head. I'm thinking about my next move when I hear someone call my name.

"Hey, Rhodeen! You deaf?"

I turn around. A cop winks at me as he slips a parking ticket under a wiper blade. Two guys walk past and smirk.

"Larson. Hi. Didn't hear you. What's up?"

"You, that's who. Parnham wants to see you."

My throat catches as I say, "What about?"

"What do you think? Play Parcheesi?"

11

PARNHAM will take it personal if I don't show up. I drive to Central and park in the lot. The building is caked in marble. In front stands four columns topped with scrollwork. A pair of marble eagles keeps watch on either side of the edifice in which *Memphis Police Station* is carved. I climb up the two sets of stairs and pull open the heavy door. The air inside is hot and dank. I walk under the rotunda and go past the Sergeant's Desk. Another cop I know is untying his shoes. A can of foot powder is on the floor.

"Hey, Regis," I say.

The cop looks up as he takes off his shoe.

"Well, Tommy Rhodeen. Maybe you heard? Stubbins and I brought in Len Jerrold and his eldest boy, Woodson, this morning. We found four hot cars in a barn next to their property. Len says he don't know nothing about them cars. Imagine that?"

"Well, Regis," I say, "it sounds like you did some good police work." The cop sprinkles some powder in his shoe. I crouch down so I can lower my voice and ask, "Hey, you know why Parnham wants to see me?"

Regis smiles. He doesn't nod or anything. I smile back, stand up, and walk down the hall. At least I know something: I should talk with Len the next time I'm looking for a stolen car.

The door is open, I look inside. Detective Parnham sits at his desk. He flips through photos from a crime scene and eats pistachios from a paper bag.

I walk in, stand in front of Parnham, and watch him eat. He doesn't look up. He splits open another pistachio and says, "Sit down, Rhodeen," as he tosses the shell into an ashtray. He looks over and indicates a chair by an empty desk. I wheel it around. The detective doesn't speak. All I hear is his breathing. He wipes his forehead with a handkerchief, sets down the photos, looks up and says, "Pistachio?"

I smile. He shoves the bag toward me. I reach in, pull out a few, and crack one open. Then Parnham takes the bag and gets some more. He brushes bits of shell from his vest and leans back.

"Know why you're here?" he says.

I throw the shell in the ashtray, toss the pistachio in my mouth and say, "I haven't the slightest idea."

Parnham looks at me and frowns. He knows I know what he means. He leans over his desk and pushes aside the bag of pistachios. He puts on his tough-guy cop voice and says, "Look Rhodeen, I can make things rough for you. The cases you do. The recovery thing? Technically, you're selling stolen merchandise. That's not me, that's the law. I know your customers want their stuff back and they're not particular how they get it. But now one wants to file a complaint, claiming you're in cahoots with some thieves."

"Yeah, who said that?"

Parnham narrows his eyes and makes a face.

"Can't say. Besides, I got him to hold off pressing charges."

I crack open another pistachio. The shell and the meat split into dust.

"Anything else?" I say.

"Yeah, just because you got a judge back his dog

doesn't make you untouchable. And, besides, Buchanan plans to retire the end of the year."

I don't speak. I reach across his desk and take a handful of pistachios.

Parnham goes back to his photos.

"Okay, you've been told. Get out of here."

I stand up and say, "Thanks for the nuts."

12

I TRY TO FORGET about Parnham as I get ready for my date with Evelyn. I shower, shave, and get dressed. I have a half hour to get to the car lot.

Evelyn and Trip are closing up as I pull in. I say hello and they hello me back. Trip drapes his arm over my shoulder. A cold expression plays across his face.

"Now, son, you get my daughter home by eleven."

I say, "Yes, sir," and nod my head.

"And no funny stuff," Trip says as if he hasn't said enough.

I should have known he was her daddy. They begin to laugh and so do I. I promise Trip I'll get Evelyn home in time, and we get in my car.

"Why didn't you warn me?" I ask.

"I thought you knew."

I shake my head and said, "No, I guess I didn't," as I pull into traffic. Then I laugh and so does Evelyn. I like her. She smells nice, too.

We drive south on Bellevue. Soon I pull into Leonard's. We go inside and sit at a booth. A waitress takes our orders.

Evelyn smiles and says, "So what do you do when you're not tracking down a Ford Thunderbird?"

"Lots of things."

"Like?"

"Well, I play guitar. I've recorded some songs and got a little airplay."

"You're a recording star?"

"I aim to be. But for now I got other business."

"What kind of business?"

"I'm a private investigator. When someone loses something and the police can't help them, they call me. I look for it and get it back."

"That's why you're looking for that car?"

"Not so much the car, but the car's owner."

Evelyn raises an eyebrow and says, "Sounds mysterious."

I smile and nod my head.

"Okay, so how'd you get into this?"

I place my palm on the back of my neck, turn my head and say, "Oh, that's kind of embarrassing."

Evelyn reaches over, takes my chin in her hand, and turns my face around.

"Embarrassing, how?"

I take her hand off my chin and hold it in mine.

"After I got out of the army, I did a bit of shade tree mechanic work. I'd just fixed this Oldsmobile. It was a '48. It'd been rear-ended twice, so it wasn't worth much. But it still drove. And this guy must have been watching because… Oh, this is embarrassing. I had to go. I mean, you know, answer the call of nature. So I went in the house and I hear the car start up. Like a dummy, I'd left the key in the ignition."

Evelyn laughs, I keep on telling the story.

"So I look out the window and, sure enough, I see that Oldsmobile speeding away. I call the police and report it. But I'm so mad I jump in my car and go looking for the fella who stole it. Well, four hours later I find him. He's got the car hid, and I don't have any proof to call the cops, so I make a deal to buy it back. I'm so happy I drive the car to the owner and tell him it's fixed. Which it was.

But I don't tell him what happened.

"So Bob Dellsmith—that's the owner of the car—drives me home. I plan to call the police as soon as I get in to tell them I got the car back. But my Aunt Norma's on the phone. And you know how that is. Bob gets pulled over four blocks later.

"Well, then the whole story comes out. People start talking about it. I had been thinking about starting my own garage, getting a proper place and all. But instead, I end up in the recovery business. And like they say, the rest is history."

We both crack up. Evelyn squeezes my hand. The waitress comes with our food. I swallow a bite of barbecue and say, "So tell me about you."

"I work for my daddy, as you know. I do the books, send the bills, write the checks, order parts and supplies. Pretty much everything but turn a wrench."

"I could teach you that."

Evelyn's eyes light up as she says, "I just might take you up on that. So what about your daddy? Tell me about your people."

I push some beans around my plate.

"Well, there's just me and my Aunt Norma. She moved in to take care of me and my daddy when I was seven. And my daddy died four years ago. He had lung cancer. That's when I was overseas. So now it's just the two of us."

"I'm sorry."

"That's okay. I also got a cousin in Nashville. On my momma's side."

We each go back to our barbecue. I eat a few bites, wash it down, and clear my throat.

"My daddy kind of did what you do," I say. "He did the accounting at the W.T. Grants."

Evelyn stops eating and looks at me. I hadn't thought about it in ages. I didn't know what I was going to say.

"My daddy grew up thinking he'd run the family interests, but after the Depression there wasn't much left. So he had to find himself a job. He found one at Grants. But after the Japs bombed Pearl Harbor, he joined the marines and fought in the Pacific. He got wounded and lost a leg. He came home and went back to Grants. Least they hired him back."

We each took a bite of our food. I wish I hadn't brought that up. I want to change the subject. Evelyn seems to sense it. She looks at her plate.

"I'm working on a big job now," I say. "For the Williamses. Claire and Garland Williams."

Evelyn looks up and sets down her fork.

"Garland Williams? He's a big shot. Wow, what on Earth are they missing?"

"Their girl, Helen. She owns that Thunderbird. She ran away and they want me to find her."

"Ran away?"

"Yeah, she and her momma don't get on. Helen's into rock 'n' roll, so they called me."

"I've seen her." Evelyn says. "It was last year. I was walking past Ellis Auditorium. Garland and Helen came out shouting at each other. In public. Can you believe?"

"What about?" I ask.

"No idea. Helen was smirking. Garland was furious. And that wife of his looked like she could spit."

"Well, he's willing to pay a lot to get her back."

We finish our barbecue, have some pie, and take a drive over to Main Street. As we walk through the crowd, I ask Evelyn about her family. She tells me her brother, Billy, was in the marines and served in Korea.

"Billy wrote us letters. Telling us what he saw and how

he felt. About fighting the KPA. He wrote that when they got into Seoul, the combat got so close they could see the expressions on the gooks' faces. It was fierce fighting, but Billy wrote that they'd be home by Christmas. But all that changed when they got above the 38th parallel. Against the Chinks, they were outnumbered. They were low on ammunition, starving, and freezing."

Evelyn rubs her eyes, and I know where the story's going.

"They got pinned down at Koto-ri," she says.

Evelyn stops speaking. She stops walking and looks at the pavement. Then she raises her head and continues. "Billy set up cover for the men. He didn't come home."

Evelyn leans into me. I put my arms around her. People walk past us. The light changes and we cross the street. I can sense Evelyn wants to talk about something else, and she asks how I learned guitar. I tell her about Dan Turner.

"When I was a kid, Dan worked for my daddy. He was the colored man who took care of the kitchen garden and did other chores around the yard. Dan played guitar after work. He made it look easy, so I asked him to teach me."

We stand in front of a movie theater. The flashing neon from the marquee lights Evelyn's hair as she pulls a thread off my shoulder.

"Dan put his guitar in my hands and taught me," I tell her. "Three months later, my daddy caught us."

"What happened?"

"He got angry. More than I'd ever seen him."

Evelyn takes hold of my hand. I haven't thought about what happened to Dan and me in years. Then a voice shouts and we turn to find a man in a black suit standing behind us. He holds a Bible in his right hand and he begins to preach.

"For there is one God and one mediator between God and men, and that man is Jesus Christ. Amen!"

People stop on the sidewalk to see what's happening. The man keeps shouting as the crowd forms.

"For it is good in the sight of God. Our Savior will save all men! All men that come to the knowledge of the truth of our Lord Jesus Christ!"

Cars stop in the street. The people lean out the windows. Evelyn clutches my hand and tries to pull me away. His eyes blaze, sweat drips from his face, and his left hand turns into a fist.

"But let the woman!" he shouts. "The woman learn in silence with all subjection!"

Two cops come running. They grab the street preacher, but he fights back. He strikes one on the nose. Blood runs over the cop's lips. The fighting stops, the cop wipes the blood off his face. Outraged, they knock the preacher down and kick him in the ass. He rolls on the concrete and continues to shout his sermon.

"I suffer not a woman to teach. Nor to usurp authority over man, but to be in silence! For Adam was first formed—"

Two more cops come. They yank the preacher to his feet and pull his arms behind his back. He twirls to avoid the handcuffs as he resumes his exhortation. His voice raises and lowers in volume, like an air-raid siren spinning, as he whirls round and round.

"For Adam was first formed. Then Eve! And Adam was not deceived! But woman deceived was… in the transgression! Notwithstanding… She shall be saved in childbearing!"

They get the cuffs on him. People cheer. A man runs out of the crowd and smashes him in the mouth with something. The police rush the preacher into the back of a squad car. He thrusts his bloody face against the glass and howls. Evelyn presses her eyes into my chest and sobs. Someone calls my name. I turn my head and see Officer Larson pick up his hat and dust himself off.

"What a show," he says.

Then he points to the theater and says, "Better than what they're showing there."

But the cop loses his grin when he realizes Evelyn is crying. "Is she okay?" he asks.

"I think she'll be. He upset her. Who wouldn't be?"

"That Reverend Dourif's crazy. This is the third time he's done this. I'll see you later, Tommy."

The cop walks away, and I hold Evelyn in my arms. People go into the theater, the traffic moves in the street. She stops crying and looks up at me.

"You all right?" I ask.

"I'm okay."

"I'm sorry you had to see that."

"It wasn't your fault. But it's kind of late. Can we go see a movie another time?"

We head back to my car. I drive Evelyn home and walk her to the door.

"I wish that didn't happen," I say as we step onto the porch. "I've never seen anyone do something like that downtown."

Evelyn wipes her eyes, they reflect under the light, and she tries to smile.

"I know. Other than that, everything was nice and I enjoyed being with you."

I move to give her a kiss. She turns her head and gives me her cheek.

"I better go in."

"I'll call you again."

"I'd like that."

She opens the door and steps inside.

"Goodnight."

"Goodnight, Evelyn."

In the car, I no longer think about the street preacher. I think about the letters Evelyn's brother wrote. My daddy never told me how he earned his medals. He wouldn't talk about the war, not even with his friends. And hearing Evelyn talk about her brother reminded me how insignificant my time in the military was.

13

DAN'S FACE, lit up in the afternoon sun, shows pure joy and he makes me feel older and stronger than my twelve years. The guitar seems like a live animal against my chest. I feel the vibrations from each note rumble through my body.

"Bend that note. Yeah. That's right. You doin' it, Tommy. Sound like a train whistle. Now, first string open. Now, second string open. Now back to the E-shuffle. Use your thumb on the down and your pointer on the up. Muffle the string with your arm on the down. Drive that guitar. Drive that guitar like a freight train. Feel that sound and let it go deep inside you. Yeah. That's the blues guitar, Tommy! Okay, now back to your train whistle! Bend that note. Yeah, Tommy!"

"Tommy!"

My father stands in front of us. His face is red. He glares at me. I've never seen him this mad, it scares me.

"Get in the house!"

I hand Dan his guitar. I stand up and my daddy slaps me across the face.

"Now get in the house before I really whack you!"

I cry. My cheek feels raw. I know I'll feel worse. I turn around and walk inside. I shut the door, peer through the window, and I see my daddy rage over Dan. Then Dan gets up with his guitar—I don't think he says a thing—and walks away. The sun is low, and I see him walk toward it. I watch behind the glass as he goes away. Dan's shadow, too, disappears. I know I'll never see him again.

My daddy stands with hands on his hips, his back to the house, the sun in his face. He stands there as if he is carved out of stone. My face hurts from the slap, but not as bad as how I feel inside. I watch my daddy bend down on his one good leg. He scoops up a handful of soil and lets it fall to the ground. The dirt, lit by the sun, looks like gold dust falling from his hands. He lifts himself up. I watch until he is about to turn around. Then I run through the kitchen and up the stairs and down the hall. I dive onto my bed. I hear the door open and slam shut. Pipes groan, and water runs through the kitchen taps. My daddy's footsteps come up the stairs; the sound is uneven from his wooden leg. He walks down the hall, into his room, and closes the door.

I open my eyes and sit up in bed. I haven't dreamed about Dan since I was a kid. Now I seem to dream or think about him all the time. The phone rings. I run down the hall to get it. It's a guy asking if I am looking for a Chevy Bel Air. I'm not. But I tell him in a week I might and to try me again. I get dressed and go downstairs. Aunt Norma already ate her breakfast. She fries eggs and bacon for me, and smokes a cigarette as I eat.

"This Evelyn, what's she like?"

"You'd like her," I say. "She's not one of those frivolous girls. She works for her daddy, he's a car dealer. Evelyn does the bookkeeping along with managing the place. Making sure the bills are paid and all."

"Humph."

"What do you mean, humph?"

"Bookkeeper? That's what your daddy did."

I set down my coffee and stare at the old bird. Bookkeeper? He was more than that. Aunt Norma pretends not to notice my expression as she wipes away the crumbs on the oilcloth where there wasn't any.

"Pretty?"

"What do you think?"

Aunt Norma smiles at me, and I take a mouthful of toast.

"Well, I got to go," she says. "Cora tried to change a light bulb, bless her heart. I'm going to drop off a covered dish and help out a while."

She comes around the table and kisses the top of my head.

"There's another green bean casserole. You have some when you get hungry. I don't know when I'll be back."

I nod and say, "There was a street preacher last night. In front of Loews."

Aunt Norma raises her eyebrows and waits for me to explain.

"He came out of nowhere, he did. Shouting Bible verses. New Testament. I think one of the epistles. And then the cops came. There was a scuffle and someone hit the guy in the face with a bottle or something."

She sets the casserole back on the counter, then turns around and puts a hand to her cheek.

"Well that's something you don't see every day. What did your Evelyn think?"

"He frightened her."

"Did he?"

"Yeah, he was crazy."

Aunt Norma chuckles, then stops herself.

"When I was a girl we used to see them like that. At revival meetings mostly. Homespun preachers and snake handlers that come out of the hills. From out near Chattanooga, I guess. Real hillbillies. Talking about how they shall take up serpents, and that they shall not get hurt. That they shall lay their hands upon the sick. That sort of stuff."

I shake my head.

"Really, you saw all that?"

"Why sure, a lot of people come watch. I think they just wanted to see if any of them get bit."

"Did they?"

"Not that I ever saw."

Aunt Norma says goodbye and leaves with the casserole. I dump my dishes in the sink with the others and open the paper. On the front page is a story about the Secretary of Defense testifying before Congress. They want to know whether America or the Soviet Union has the lead for nuclear air power supremacy. I read another article. It's about Eisenhower signing the Federal Aid Highway Act. I turn to the local section and spot a headline that stops me cold.

Williams's Chauffeur Missing

I read the story.

> Albert Cuffee, the chauffeur of Mr. and Mrs. Garland Williams, was reported missing after the car he drove for them was found abandoned along U.S. Route 72, a little more than halfway between Slayden and Walnut, Mississippi. The car, a 1956 Cadillac Eldorado, was undamaged and, according to police reports, no clues were recovered at the scene. Cuffee, age 47, was last seen on Wednesday, June 27 driving Mr. Williams home from the Tennessee Club.
>
> Investigating the case is Lieutenant Joseph J. Fessenden, who stated that Mr. Williams had told Cuffee to return a rare book to a private

collector. Cuffee never arrived with the book, nor did he return to the Williams's home at the end of day. Lieutenant Fessenden says they have no suspects and are treating it as a missing person case. The chauffeur's wife, Gladys Cuffee, a domestic, age 44, says she has no knowledge of her husband's whereabouts or of him having any enemies. They have six children, ranging in age from seven to eighteen.

According to Mr. Williams, the book Cuffee had in his possession is a rare manuscript...

I toss the paper and get dressed. I drive to the Williamses. I knock on the door. The butler answers.

"Is Mr. or Mrs. Williams in? I'd like to speak with them. It's about Mr. Cuffee."

The butler speaks while avoiding my eyes.

"Mrs. Claire's out. Yes, she's out. I'll go see if Mr. Garland can speak with you."

He lets me into the foyer and closes the door. I wait. I'm not sure what I'm going to say. He comes back before I've had a chance to think.

"This way please, Mr. Tommy."

The butler leads me to the library. He knocks once and opens the door. Mr. Williams sits behind his desk.

"What is it, Mr. Rhodeen?"

"I read about your driver, Albert Cuffee."

Mr. Williams closes a book and says, "I can't understand why Albert vanished. He's always been dependable. I had placed great trust in him. I told the police the same thing."

"How long has he worked for you?"

"Twenty-two years. The last seven as a driver."

"And nothing like this has ever happened before?"

"Never. What are you getting at?"

"There could be a connection."

"A connection?"

"Just that there might be more to the story."

"Meaning?"

"I visited your cabin. Twice. You told me your driver checked it out, and that no one had been there. I saw otherwise."

"What are you implying?"

"That Albert Cuffee may have known something he didn't tell you."

Mr. Williams's face grows red.

"Mr. Rhodeen, you understand I hired you to find my missing daughter, not my driver. The police have their work to do and you have yours."

"Two people missing from the same household? What are the odds?"

"They are not worth playing. I will ask you to refrain from bringing the whereabouts of my chauffeur into your investigation. I already told you, I don't want any undue attention regarding my daughter. Are you prepared to hold up your end of our agreement?"

I tell him what he wants to hear, but his reaction only adds to my suspicions. The butler shows me out and I drive a world away from Morningside Place. I need to pay a call on Harold P. Washington.

Harold had connections with 'Sunbeam' Mitchell and 'Hardface' Clanton. He provided entertainment for their nightclubs, musical and otherwise. Harold was also a bit of a fixer and the two of us did business from time to time, as it benefited each of us to have an ally with different colored skin.

He first called me when a cousin of his lost a carload of untaxed cigarettes driven in from North Carolina.

Some white boys stopped the car outside of town. They took the car and the cigarettes, and left the two coloreds to hoof it to a phone booth. I brokered the deal. His cousin got back the cigarettes and the car. That I made it happen didn't surprise Harold. That I didn't take a fee did, but I genuinely like the man so it was more than merely good will.

I park across the street from Harold's office. I get out and I'm the only white man on the sidewalk. I ignore the stares and keep going. His office is above a liquor store on Beale Street. The door to the stairwell is open. I go in. There's enough daylight to climb the stairs. The runner is loose and some of the stair sticks are missing. The second floor hallway is dimly lit. I walk past two office doors with no names on them. On the third, stenciled in gold paint on the frosted glass, is *Harold P. Washington, Promoter*. Harold's Mississippi accent floats through the transom.

I knock.

"Come in."

I step into the reception area. On the walls are old posters for some of the singers and bands Harold used to work with. He smiles when he sees it's me and says, "I'll call you back," into the phone. He hangs up and comes from around the desk.

"Tommy, good to see you!"

I shake his hand.

"You don't look so good," he says. "What's up?"

"Where's Lotte?" I ask to avoid getting right down to as why I'd come.

"She had to go run an errand. Let's go to my office."

He leads me into the next room. On the wall above Harold's desk are photographs of the singers he used to manage. Harold has come far for the stepson of a sharecropper; a petty man who took out his frustrations on a boy because he showed aptitude and interest beyond farming. Harold motions me to sit and opens the file cabinet. He comes up with a bottle and two glasses. We have a drink. I offer him a cigarette. Then Harold sits back in his chair to signal he's ready to hear why I came.

"I'm working a missing person job," I say. "A spoiled girl from Morningside Place. She and her family don't get on."

Harold blows a cloud of smoke over my head.

"Morningside Place? That's way out of my territory. Why talk to me?"

"I read in the paper that the family's driver is missing. It looks like he was—"

Harold holds up the *Tri-State Defender*.

"Albert Cuffee."

"Yes. Albert Cuffee. The story doesn't sit right."

"You read the *Press-Scimitar* or the *Commercial Appeal* so you don't know the half of it."

Harold shakes the paper, making it pop.

"According to this, Cuffee's missing because he was accused of raping a white woman. No evidence, mind you, and the po-lice won't say nothing. But with Fessenden on it, you might as well forget all about seeing Cuffee again."

He stabs the paper with his finger.

"Says here, Cuffee is all of five foot two inches tall and weighs 124 pounds. Now I never met the man myself, but this puny nigger hardly seems *the image of a big buck Negro and a menace to white femininity*."

I set down my glass and say, "I asked his employer about him. Mr. Williams said he was loyal. Worked for him twenty-two years. Always placed great trust in him."

"He tell that to the po-lice?"

"He says he did. I asked him something else. I asked if there might be a connection between Cuffee missing and his missing daughter."

Harold nods and takes a drag on his cigarette.

"Garland Williams didn't react how a father should," I say.

"You suspect something's up?"

"I want to speak with Cuffee's wife."

Harold laughs and says, "That all?"

I nod. He pulls open a drawer and tosses me the Memphis city directory.

"Look 'em up, mister private investigator."

I thumb through the pages. Harold hands me a pad. I write down the information. He crushes out his cigarette and says, "You want me to go with you, right?"

A smile creeps across my face.

14

WE TAKE MY CAR to North Memphis. Harold sits up front and after a while he says, "You hear that one about Saint Peter and the colored kid?"

"No. Can't say I have."

"Well, Saint Peter looks down at this skinny little colored boy outside his gates. Little slip of a kid. About eight years old, and Saint Peter says, 'What you doin' here, boy?'

"The kid looks up. He's all nervous and says, 'I must of died, suh.'

"'Died? What the Hell's your name, boy?'

"The kid says, 'Russell, suh.'

"'Russell? You gotta last name, Russell?'

"'Yessuh. It's Green.'

"So Saint Peter puts on his reading glasses and he thumbs through his book. And he says, 'Russell Green. You're not on my list. In fact, your name's nowhere here a'tall. You sure you're supposed to be here?'

"The boy shrugs his shoulders and says 'I don't know, suh. I guess so.'

"Saint Peter hooks his thumbs in his belt and says, 'You guess so? Well I need to know something about you, boy, before I let you go on into Paradise. Not just anyone can come off the street and pass through these Pearly Gates. You understand what I'm saying, boy?'

"Well, Russell nods his head and says, 'Yessuh.'

"'Okay, Russell, you tell me this. You do anything bad?

You steal or cuss?'

"He shakes his head and says, 'Nosuh'

"'So you're a good boy, Russell. Tell me something good you done do.'

"The boy thinks and thinks and then he says, 'Well, my momma's boyfriend was yelling and beating on her so I go on up to him and I say, 'You lay another hand on my momma, you gotta go through me.'

"Saint Peter steps back and looks down at this runty-ass little nigger and says, 'You said that? Damn, boy, when did all this happen?'

"'About two minutes ago.'"

Harold laughs and slaps the dashboard of the car. Truth is, I know all about Harold's upbringing. He could easily have been that kid, and probably came close to it on more than a few occasions.

"Yeah," I say as I shake my head. "I'll have to remember that one."

We pull up in front of the house. The Cuffees live in a brick duplex. A wire fence borders a yard in which a bunch of children play. We get out of my car and walk through the gate. Harold knocks as he opens the screen door and we step inside.

A room full of colored faces turns toward me. I feel out of place. I see Mrs. Cuffee sitting in a shabby chair surrounded by her people. She's in her middle-forties and appears lean and strong. Her blue-black skin reflects the light from a table lamp and her eyes are red and sore.

I walk to her and say, "Mrs. Cuffee, my name's Tommy Rhodeen. I'm sorry to hear about your husband."

"Do I know you?"

"No, I was hired by the Williamses. I want to ask you some questions about your husband."

She nods her head and sits forward.

"Did anyone have anything against Albert? Was there any reason why someone would want to harm him?"

"Albert? Why he never hurt nobody. And he no way did what some folks are saying. Had a bad back. He was no big thing. Why would anyone want to do something to Albert?"

"I don't know," I say. "But this story doesn't seem right. How did he get on with the Williamses?"

"Why they'se good people. Albert worked for them more'n twenty years. They say they gonna take good care of me and my chilen. That's what they say."

"I'm glad to hear that."

Several people begin to whisper. Two women come forward and they get between Mrs. Cuffee and me. The first woman puts her hands on her hips.

"What you say you doing here?"

I try to stay cool as I tell her, "I'm working on another job for the Williamses, and I think there might be a connection."

The second woman sticks her finger in my face.

"Another job? Then you is not exactly here to do somethin' 'bout what happened to Albert. Are you?"

She makes me mad, but I try not to show it. I keep my voice level as I blurt out, "I hope that by learning what happened I can find out what took place."

It wasn't quite the words I meant to say. The room falls silent. The first woman gives me a malignant look; she turns toward Mrs. Cuffee and tells her, "Gladys, you don't need to say nothing to this peckerwood. He probably thinks Albert stole that old book."

I was about to say something when Harold steps forward.

"Now hold on. This white boy don't mean no harm. He got a job to do and it may be the best chance you got.

Think on it. You think the po-lice are going to find out what happened to Albert? Hell, no."

Harold pulls me out of the way, which is fine by me, and he keeps talking:

"Right now you just wants to be angry. And you're angry at the wrong peoples."

There's murmuring after that. Mrs. Cuffee gets up and walks across the room. She bends down in front of an old woman. Her brown skin looks like wrinkled paper; she sits low in a ragged easy chair, the cloth all worn and stained with oil spots.

"What you think, momma?" she asks.

The old woman raises her chin and says, "Girl, you haven't asked me what I think since you was nine years old. 'Bout time you did. You think these girlfriends of yours gonna help you find your man?"

She points at the one who called me a peckerwood.

"That Angela there had least two men run off on her and leave her with a whole mess of chilen, and you gonna listen to what she says? This white boy? I don't know if he gonna help or not, but I know these others sure ain't. Now I'm tired. I'm going to take a nap. You do what you want. Besides, you gonna do it anyways."

She pushes herself out of the chair and walks into the next room. Everyone else looks back and forth between Mrs. Cuffee and us. There's nothing more we can say. Harold and I make our apologies. We say goodbye and leave.

"What do you think?" I ask Harold as we reach my car.

"I sure like her momma. Just wish she'd spoke up about ten or twenty years sooner. But, sheeit, no one there knows the truth, or if they is they ain't telling."

"We're on the same page," I say.

I drive Harold back to his office before I go home. I have no idea if Albert's disappearance has anything to do with Helen's, but there has to be more to the story.

*   *   *

Later that night, I drive to the Eagle's Nest. I walk in, pay a buck, and climb up to the second floor. Eddie Bond and his Stompers are on the stage. Some dancers turn on the floor. I don't recognize the guy behind the bar.

"Where's Roy?" I ask. He can't hear with the band playing and I have to ask him again.

"Hospital. Had to get his appendix out. You want a beer?"

I nod my head and say, "Yeah, and some fries."

He hands me a beer and I watch the band from the bar. More people come in. I wait until the bartender isn't busy. I show him the photo of Helen. He tells me he's only been working there a few nights and knows nothing about her. I drink my beer. More people look at the photo. Two think they recognize her, but can't say for sure.

Charlie Feathers waves to me from the door. I motion him to come over. He slaps me on the back. I show him the photo. Charlie knows her. He tells me Helen had tried to make a date with him, but he told her to get lost. He thinks it's funny I'm getting paid to look for her.

"You couldn't pay me enough to be in the same room with her," Charlie says and laughs. I shake my head and get another beer.

Eddie and his guys clear the stage, then Charlie and his band set up. Eddie comes over to the bar and I show him Helen's photo. He thinks she looks familiar, but isn't certain; he does say she looks real pretty. I don't tell Eddie what Charlie said about her. I finish my beer as I watch Charlie and his band play; no one else sounds quite like him. I hang around until he finishes his set. That way the night won't be so much of a loss.

It's late when I pull into the driveway. The porch light's on and two moths orbit around it. I go in. Aunt Norma left me some fried chicken along with some biscuits and beans. I get a plate and pour myself a glass of milk. I sit down and eat. Footsteps pad down the stairs. I turn around and say, "Sorry, did I wake you?" to Aunt Norma as she comes into the kitchen.

"No, I was up. I just came down to see you and get a glass of water. You getting anywhere finding this girl?"

"I don't know. Not really, I guess."

"Did you ever go talk with Arthur Groom about his garage? He told me he'd might agree to let you pay it off over time. No down payment. He thinks you're a fine mechanic."

I use my tongue to rub some chicken out from between my teeth and upper lip.

"You know that's not what I see for myself."

"Well, what do you see for yourself?"

"I don't know. Not that. Music, I guess."

"Music, you guess?"

She looks at me and waits for me to say something. I take a drink of milk and say, "I saw Harold Washington today."

"Now what are you doing seeing him? You just want to get into more trouble?"

"Harold helped me see the wife of Mr. Williams's chauffeur. He's missing, too."

Aunt Norma sighs and says, "Sounds like more trouble to me."

I wipe my plate with a biscuit as I tell her, "You just don't like Harold."

"I don't think of Harold one way or the other. I'm just thinking of you."

"Yeah, well…"

Aunt Norma picks up my plate and sets it into the sink. She turns to me as she washes her hands and says, "Well, as far as the garage, why don't you just sleep on it?"

I finish my milk and get up.

"I'm going to bed, goodnight."

"You'll think on it?"

"Goodnight."

"We'll talk on it more later."

"Goodnight."

15

PATIENT VISITING HOURS are from one to four. I get there after three. I lean against the car and smoke a cigarette. Building this hospital was the dying wish of a rags-to-riches hotelier—a French immigrant named John Gaston who settled in Memphis and fought for the Confederacy—but inside is grim and what you'd expect from a charity hospital.

As a philanthropist, John Gaston was as noble as they come. But he had some interesting ideas when it came to marriage. He married his stepdaughter—the daughter of his departed wife—after his first wife died. I shake my head and wonder if Mr. Williams would marry his step-daughter, Helen, should anything happen to Claire? That assumes I find her first.

I crush my cigarette under my shoe as I hold open the heavy door. A couple my age walk out of the hospital holding hands with their little boy, a relieved look shows on their faces as they walk into the sunlight.

I step inside. A nurse tells me where to go. I follow her directions to the third floor. I walk down the hall and peek in the ward. I find Roy with the others. Some have visitors, most do not. The room smells like urine and disinfectant. I walk in. An old man looks up at me. He opens his mouth as if to say something; his eyes bare a confused expression as if I might be a relation whose name he can't recall. I pause and shake my head before I continue past some other patients. Roy lies on his back in the hospital bed, counting the tiles on the ceiling.

"Roy, how you feeling?" I call out.

He turns his head and smiles.

"Tommy! Hey, am I glad to see you."

I tell him I am too, and I ask him again how he feels.

"My guts hurt and I can't take a shit to save my life," he says and starts to laugh. He winces and stops.

"So how are you?" Roy asks. "You haven't been by the club in a while. Hey, how'd you know I was here, anyway?"

"I came by last night. The guy tending bar told me."

Roy motions for me to bend closer and whispers, "You didn't bring me a beer and some fries? The food here's something awful."

I close my eyes and wish I'd brought something.

"That's okay," Roy says. "I'm just glad to see you."

"I could go get something and come back. What would you like?"

"No, that's okay. I'm fine. I'll be getting out of here in a couple of days."

"It wouldn't be any trouble."

"No, Tommy. I'm okay."

Part of me wants to leave Helen's photo in my pocket. I don't want Roy to think I came only because I needed something from him. But I'd have kicked myself if he knows where Helen's gone and I didn't ask. I take out the photo and set it on the bed.

"Do you know her?"

Roy picks it up and scratches his chin.

"Can't remember her name, but she used to come in all the time."

I try to jog his memory and say, "Her name's Helen. Helen Williams."

"Helen. Yes. Helen Williams. I saw this here girl say

she was going to Nashville to get married."

"Nashville?"

"Yeah, to get married."

"When was that?"

"Friday, the week before last."

"You sure it was her?"

Roy hands me the photo.

"Absapositively."

16

IT'S TWO YEARS since I'd been to Nashville. I get up at five to get an early start. That would put me there before ten. I'll look up my cousin, Donald, when I get there. He knows music and might have some ideas on where I should look for Helen.

Just outside Memphis, I stop at a diner. There's a gravel lot to the side of the place. I drive past the rigs and park. I walk in and take a seat at the counter one spot over from where Jim Gantry sits holding a cup of coffee. We ignore each other. I study the menu. He reads the paper.

The waitress sets down a plate with a single large pancake in front of Jim; it comes with a big pat of butter. She refills his coffee and pours me mine. Jim tilts the bottle of syrup. He pours it until the pancake can't absorb another drop. He cuts a piece from the center of the plate and forks it into his mouth.

I look up. The waitress taps a pencil on her pad; I order breakfast. She walks away, tears off the paper, and clips it into the order wheel hanging in the pass through. A cook sets down a plate of eggs, rings the bell, and pulls my order.

Alone, I swivel in my seat and say, "Hey Jim," to the tall man in blue dungarees, plaid shirt, and cowboy boots. Jim raises his cup. He holds it there and stares over it as if he's reading the specials on the wall. A second or two passes. He says, "Tommy," takes a sip, and sets the cup down. I swivel back in my seat and mutter, "Heading to Nashville," between my teeth.

"That so? Business or pleasure?"

"Business."

Jim cuts another bite.

"You need another loan?"

"No, but can you fix me up?" I say out the corner of my mouth.

"You got cash?"

"Yes."

"Can do."

Jim eats his pancake. He works his way out from the center—forming an atoll in a sea of buttery syrup—until the only thing left on his plate is a maple slick.

The waitress says, "Here you go honey," and sets down a plate in front of me. I spread jelly on my toast and stab my eggs with a fork. Jim goes back to reading the paper. Two truckers nod at him as they leave the diner. The waitress refills our coffee. She leans over me; her breast rubs against my shoulder. I finish eating and pay for my meal.

I go into the men's room and clean my hands. The door swings open as I pull the loop of towel from the box on the wall. Jim checks if anyone's in the stall. I set my money on the edge of the sink. Jim picks up the cash. He takes a small plastic bag full of pills from his jacket and places it where the money had been. I pick up the bennies. No words are spoken. I leave and get back in my car.

I arrive in Nashville a little past ten thirty. Perched on top of a building are a smokestack and a water tower. *Neuhoff Packing Company* is painted on its side. The slaughterhouse is built on a bluff overlooking the Cumberland River. Over time, it's become a compound containing a number of two- and four-story buildings all constructed of rose-colored brick. I drive through the gates and park. The pens are full of hogs, cattle, noise, and dust. Green-eyed flies buzz about. I walk through the soot and cinders, open a door, and scan about for my cousin. A fella walks past me with several briskets draped over his shoulder. I ask another guy for Donald. He points toward the back. There I find him working over a carcass.

"Tommy! What are you doing here?"

"Looking for a girl."

"In Neuhoff's?"

"No, just Nashville."

"Well, that narrows it down," he says. "Who is she?"

I show him the photo and say, "Helen Williams. She comes from money. Likes rock 'n' roll. Came here to get married."

Donald looks at it and gives me a shrug.

"Why are you looking for her?"

"Her parents hired me to."

"Good a reason as any."

Donald rubs his chin and shakes his head.

"You say this girl like that rock and roll music? She's gonna be none too happy here."

"Why's that?"

"This ain't Memphis. There's not many places that go in for that kind of music. What you got here's swing bands, pop, and hillbilly music."

"No rock 'n' roll?"

"Maybe one or two spots. The Subway or the Subway Club? Something like that. Over on Fourth across from the Noel Hotel. But they might be more pop, come to think of it."

Maybe Roy made a mistake. He seemed pretty sure he recognized Helen and heard her say she's going to

Nashville. Maybe it wasn't so much the music she likes, but any place she could go have fun.

"Are the honky tonks still on Lower Broad?"

Donald grins and says, "Yeah, that's where they are all right. How long you in town for?"

"Depends how soon I find her."

"You're welcome to spend the night. Lois and the kids would be tickled to see you."

"I'd take you up on it, but if I find her I got to bring her straight back home. Otherwise, I'll be out all night looking for her."

I thank Donald, leave, and drive south toward downtown. I get onto Fourth and pass the Noel Hotel. There's no sign for the Subway on any of the buildings, so I go into the hotel and ask. The clerk tells me the club's across the street, but no one would be there till later.

I get back in my car and head for Lower Broad. That part of Broadway's known for honky tonks, cheap hotels, and peep shows. I park my car and walk into Mom's. Photos of musicians from the Grand Ole Opry cover the walls. Mom's has become their hangout since they can go out the back door of the Ryman, cross the alley, go through the back door of Mom's, get a beer, and get back for their next set. And no one would be the wiser, unless they got plastered. Old men play cards under a layer of cigarette smoke. Mom stands behind the bar. She's in her forties and wears her hair in a bun. She looks up and goes back to rinsing glasses. I set Helen's photo on the bar.

"Any chance you seen this girl? Would have been within the past week or so. Name's Helen, but she may be going by something else."

Mom wipes off her hands, picks up the photo, and studies it a while.

"Can't say I have. She kin to you?"

I shake my head as she hands me the photo.

"No. Her folks asked me to find her. She run off looking for a good time."

Mom laughs and says, "Well, you come back tonight. You'll like as might see her."

I smile and thank her and go outside. I hear a jukebox from down the block. The door's propped open. I walk inside. The lights are on, there's no customers. A guy wipes the mirror behind the bar. He sports a faded tattoo of a mermaid on his arm. I step up to the bar and say, "Mind if I ask you a few questions?"

"Depends who's asking them?" he says as he tosses a rag into a bucket.

I show him my P.I. license.

"What do you want to know?"

I set Helen's photo on the bar.

"I'm looking for her. She's seventeen, but can pass for twenty. She came out here from Memphis. Some story about getting married. Her family wants her back."

He looks at the photo; then hollers, "Hey, Edna! Come out here."

The doors push open, and a woman appears. She clenches a cigarette between her lips. Her coarse hair hangs uncombed. It's streaked with gray. The capillaries in her nose appear shot. Her hands look raw.

"You seen this girl?" the man asks.

She puffs her cigarette without using her hands. Smoke exhales out her blackened nostrils. She picks up the photo, gives it a look, and sets it on the bar. She grunts a no. The cigarette jerks in her mouth. She opens herself a beer and goes back to the kitchen.

I thank the man, walk onto the street, and keep looking. This goes on for hours. Not a single person recognizes Helen. I feel hopeless as I go into the next bar.

It serves me right for listening to Roy and coming all the way out here, not that I can blame him.

I figure I'll try the Subway Club again now that it should be open. I get there. A few people stand around. The band has cancelled and no one has seen or heard of Helen Williams. So I turn back toward Lower Broad and walk up and down the avenues. I pass the Ryman and go into Mom's. I buy some folks a beer. No one has seen Helen. I'm hungry. I'm tired. I'm tired of talking to people. I go into a place to eat. As the man sets down the plate I ask him to look at the photo. He lifts it up, and I can see in his eyes what I'd been hoping for.

"Yeah, I've seen her. Threw her out last night. She acted like she owned the place. Pickin' fights, even."

Helen is here, in Nashville. It's just a matter of time. But now it's midnight and the bars are closing. I've put in a full day and night. I ask the guy as he puts up the chairs where I can get some sleep. He tells me to go to the Merchant's Hotel or to the rooming house around the corner.

I choose the nearer option and pay for a night. The old woman wears a shabby housecoat. She doesn't ask me my name. She takes the cash and hands me a skeleton key polished from years of use. I climb the stairs, walk down the hall, unlock the door, and feel for a switch.

A frosted bulb glows in a fixture that had once lit the room with gas. I'm tired, and the light is dim. My eyes strain to take in the place. Wallpaper curls where it meets the picture molding. There's one window, it looks over the street. I lie down on the iron bed. The springs wrench each time I move.

I flip on the light near my head. Dried-up snot and the imprint of a thumb-squashed cockroach appear on the wall. I'm too tired to care.

I'd just fallen asleep when I hear a noise from out in

the hall. It's the sound of a pair of feet slowly treading along the runner. The man sighs as he fumbles with the key. Then a door opens and closes across the hall.

Unable to get back to sleep, I get up to close the curtains. I peer out the window. Two prostitutes chat up a customer on the corner. He points at one and they cross the street. The other taps her shoe on the sidewalk. She looks up. I move away from the window.

17

A BANG AGAINST the paper-thin wall is followed by shouts and the crash of a lamp. Two guys fight in the next room; one accuses the other of stealing ten dollars. Startled from sleep, I lift my head off the pillow as I hear feet in the hallway and the sound of a passkey. A man throws the two out and onto the street. I look at my watch. It's almost seven. I feel tired, but I can't get back to sleep. I get up, go down the hall to the bathroom, and leave.

I walk into Linebaugh's for breakfast and find a spot among the old men. Afterward, I sit on the steps of the Ryman. Everything's closed. It's too early to search for Helen. I get in my car and drive to the river. I park in a lot and try to nap. I can't sleep. I get out and step through weeds and gravel and trash, and cross the tracks until I am under the shadow of the Shelby Street Bridge. I hear the clank clank of the cars and the ruffling of pigeons roosting on the girders overhead. Below, I see an old colored man in a skiff on the river. He hauls in a trotline and comes up with five or six catfish.

I take the footpath down to the water. I tread between knotted-up coils of fishing line, dog turds, and broken glass. The old man has tied up his boat. He steps onto the bank and gives me a nod as we meet.

"What are you using for bait?" I ask.

"Mostly days-old chicken livers, gizzards, and hearts. Them cats like stinky stuff."

The old man holds a catfish from behind its pectoral fins, and he sets it on a broad piece of driftwood. The cat opens and shuts its mouth and raises its spines. Then the man clubs it upside the head with the handle end of a hammer.

"You not from around here," he says.

"No, I'm from Memphis."

He mutters something, picks up a sixty-penny nail, and hammers it through the head of the fish. He uses a pair of pliers to rip the skin off the cat. After he peels it, he works the nail back and forth till he can pull it out. He grips the naked catfish and pokes the tip of his knife into its gullet. He runs the edge of the blade toward its anus, cutting a vent from which the cat's innards pour out in a wad of gore.

"So Memphis? What you doin' this aways?"

"Looking for a girl."

"She run off on you?"

"No. Nothing like that."

He makes a humph sound. Then he wipes his knife on the leg of his pants and wraps the fish in a sheet of newspaper. The old man speaks while he does the same to the rest of his catch.

"Bud, lemme tell you somethin' 'bout women. They got this sixth sense. Let's 'em see things plain as day. The problem is they think we see 'em, too. You see where I'm goin' with this?"

I smile and nod my head.

"So this girl who run off on you."

"She didn't run off on me. Her daddy hired me to find her."

The old colored man laughs as he picks up his parcel of papered cats.

"Okay, bud. I see you don't wanna be helped. That

your perogativ'. But if it was me I'd study on what this girl done see that you don't."

The fisherman shoves off in his boat. He gives me a wave and calls out, "Open your eyes, bud. Open your eyes!"

There's no point in arguing. I wave and watch him as he goes about his boat. He resets his trotline before he rows his way downriver; his oars make whirlpools in the Cumberland.

I sit on a piece of driftwood and scratch my back. The sun feels good. I close my eyes, letting the sounds of the river fill my ears. My head falls forward and I think I fell asleep. It may've only been for a few seconds. I sense a bug land and crawl on my arm. I open my eyes. I hold still thinking it's a wasp until I realize it's only a mantidfly. It takes off as I get up and wipe the dirt from my pants. I walk along the bank and look across the water to where they're building barges. One looks days away from sliding into the river. A tugboat chugs beneath the bridge, causing a squad of pigeons to take off and fly in an arc before returning to their roost. I look at my watch, turn around, and toss a stone at a snapping turtle. It falls short, but the turtle plunges off its log.

As I head up from the riverbank, I pass a ring of charred stones where hobos made their cooking fires. I turn my ankle on a loose board. I cuss and shake out my foot before I trudge up the rest of the way and cross the tracks to get back to my car. I start the engine and drive on over to Lower Broad.

18

NOW THAT more places are open, I get on with looking for Helen. I try again at Ernest Tubb's. I walk up Fifth and on over to the Arcade. I stop in at Stroebel's, then I get something to eat at a Krystal before walking back to Lower Broad. The day and much of the evening are a repeat of the day before. All I get is same string of nothings until about nine o'clock when a bartender says he'd seen Helen.

"Yeah, I've seen her. But you're too late."

"Why's that?"

"She's in the morgue. Got in a fight with some girl last night about closing time. Called her a danged something or other. What I don't know? The other one had a knife and knew how to use it."

I push the photograph closer and make him hold it.

"You sure it's her?"

"Yeah, that's her all right."

I finally find Helen, but I find her too late. I stagger out of the bar and onto the street. I see a cop on a motorcycle. I tell him I need to identify a body. He tells me how to get to the hospital as if he's giving directions to a tourist site. I get in my car and drive.

I park and walk through the double doors. The same set Helen had gone through last night, only she went through them on her back. In the waiting room an old man vomits into his lap. A mother holds a listless child with pallid skin. If it's a boy or girl, I couldn't tell. I open a door to a staircase and descend into the basement. A lone attendant is on duty. I hold out the photo of Helen.

"I'm looking for her," I say. "She'd been stabbed."

He looks at the photo.

"You the husband?"

"No, I was hired to find her."

His face remains blank, so I dig out my wallet and show him my P.I. license. The attendant nods, gets up from his desk, and beckons me to follow. Our footsteps echo on the tile. He opens a door and flips on a switch. There is a hum and a series of fluorescent tubes flicker awake on the ceiling. The greenish light reveals a room full of gurneys on a concrete floor that slopes to a drain.

We walk up to one; he pulls back the shroud and exposes her face. I look back and forth between the photo of Helen and the dead girl. I can't be sure. Maybe I just can't imagine that girl in the painting with the cat ending up in a place like this.

"Did she have identification?" I ask. "Was she wearing jewelry? A wedding band?"

He lifts a clipboard and skims the paperwork.

"Nancy Rollo. Her parents identified her at one forty-five this morning. Jewelry? Yeah. She had on a ring and a locket. It says here they signed for all that. They must be making arrangements."

I thank the man and walk away. Nancy Rollo? I have to keep searching. I need to find Helen. I couldn't have come this far for this. I walk upstairs to the waiting room. At a drinking fountain marked WHITE, I lave my forehead and dry myself off with my sleeve. I take a drink. It tastes of corroded pipes. I pop one of Jim's pills and quit the hospital.

I spend the next several hours wandering in and out of dive bars and honky tonks. I retrace my steps from the last two days. I walk along Broad, from the river to Seventh, and up and down the side streets. I talk to anyone who'll listen, but nobody's seen Helen.

I sit on the curb. I look at the bar across the street and realize I'm lost. It's as if I have walked into a different city. I close my eyes, but the sound of shouts and shattered bottles breaks my thoughts. Wild men in oil-stained coveralls and patched-up dungarees, lugging clubs and knives, approach each other. Their thin faces wear cruel expressions that bare the marks of malnutrition. I jump out of the way and ask the man next to me what it's about. He tells me the fight began years ago, the impetus long forgotten. One side comes from some meager place up in Kentucky and the other from some rundown quarter in Knoxville. Year after year, they come back to settle their score. An ugly crowd gathers and cheers till somebody fires a shot. They all scatter. A siren wails and I get moving; my shoes crunch the broken glass reflecting in the street.

Beyond the mayhem, I pass men going in and out of peep shows. I head north and wind up in Printer's Alley. I drift past the Black Poodle and the Rainbow Room, while the barkers describe the sights and the talents and the measurements within. Through the gutters and along the sidewalks flow the last of the partygoers. A man bumps into me, he pukes on my shoes. It's obvious I will not find Helen here, and this night walk has become something less than futile.

The bars close. I wander toward the river in the dark. I see the shapes of hobos and of degenerates curled up in doorways, hugging their bottles of 'splo or squeezing Sterno juice through a sock. Their eyes reflect back at me as I pass. The sound of urine splatters against the wall. The shadow of an old man turns around and exposes itself before it buttons its fly and hobbles away like a glue factory horse in search of cheaper whiskey.

I shuffle forward. A gust of wind comes up from the river. It carries the reek of muck, and it pushes forth a wave of handbills and candy wrappers and grit. It traverses along the sidewalk, until the wind dies, and the swell of detritus breaks hard upon the concrete. Two figures emerge from the gloom and they take position under the glare from a sign of a cheap hotel.

"Hey sport. You like to dance?"

She hikes her dress above a knee revealing a pair of bruised legs. Her hair is unkempt and hangs down in strings.

"No thanks."

"Come on handsome," says the other. She sets her hands on her hips and flashes a smile short a few teeth. A black eye is visible under a crust of makeup. I ignore them both.

Then the sound of the horn and the rumble of the wheels precede the flash of the headlamp as a northbound freight train labors along the tracks above the Cumberland. Its hot sulfurous breath blasts as it passes. Gnomes stare out from empty boxcars, their malevolent eyes glowing. A devilkin clutches the handrail atop a reefer. I walk on. The ground shakes harder beneath my feet until the locomotive and its load has passed.

I light a cigarette in the newborn silence and notice something low that moves in my direction. It seems to drop down in a swimming motion as it comes forward. Together we enter from opposite ends of the yellow pool of a street lamp. It looks up at me. The top half of a man propped on a roller board. It holds a pair of wooden blocks that it uses to propel itself forward. It stares into my eyes and demands a cigarette. I shuck one from my pack; it snatches the cigarette from my hand. It strikes a match, lights itself up, and pushes itself away on its wheels. Smoke trails in its wake like exhaust.

Someone laughs. I look up and see the glow of a cigarette bob up and down in an open window. I turn back toward town. The two streetwalkers no longer stand on their corner. I make for the same rooming house as the night before.

19

SOMETIME AROUND SUNRISE I fell asleep. It takes the sound of a garbage truck to wake me. I look at my watch. It's past ten. My body aches. I haul myself out of bed and stumble down the hall to the bathroom.

I go in. I open the valve on the clawfoot tub and strip off my clothes. The shower, improvised with several pieces of plumbing, vibrates unless the water pressure is set just right. I step into the filthy tub. I apply hot water and harsh soap. Two days go down the drain in a sludge of soap scum and hair. I want to forget Nashville and Helen. I think of Evelyn. I left Memphis in such a hurry I didn't tell her I was going. I dry off, go back to my room, and get dressed.

At the corner, I find a phone booth. An old, fat guy stands inside. He isn't doing much talking except for an occasional, "Okay," "All right," and "I will." He finally hangs up. I go in and call long distance. Then I put several more coins in the slot. There's a series of clicks. The phone rings. It gets picked up. A voice says, "Trip's Used Cars."

"Evelyn."

"This is she. Who is this?"

"Evelyn, it's me. Tommy. I'm in Nashville."

"Nashville? What are you doing there?"

"Looking for Helen, but I got a bum lead."

"That's too bad. You coming back?"

"Yeah, there's nothing here."

"I can't hear you so good. What did you say?"

"I said I'm coming back."

"That's great. Dad and I are going to the fireworks tonight. You want to come? If you don't have plans."

"Yeah, that'd be great. I'll be back before then."

I step out of the phone booth. I forgot it was the Fourth of July. I look for my car, get in, and drive to Donald's. I ring the bell. He opens the door.

"You find her?"

"For a moment I thought so," I say, "but it was more like her ghost."

Donald gives me a weird look.

"I ended up in the morgue last night. There was a girl. She looked like Helen, but it wasn't her."

"That's too bad—I mean, good that it wasn't her."

"I got a bum lead. I got to get back. Is Lois here?"

"No. She and the kids went on a picnic. I'm heading there now. You want to come?"

"I can't, but tell them I say hi."

"Sure will. You come for a real visit next time. Not like this. Okay?"

I tell him I will and begin the drive home. An hour later, it starts to rain. The hard rain and a straight unending road and a lack of sleep make my eyes grow heavy. It seems as if the car is driving in place. Like I'm in neutral and the engine spins free out of gear.

There's little traffic. I think about Evelyn and, if the rain stops, how nice it'll be to go with her to the fireworks. Maybe her dad will find an excuse to stay home, or he'll go watch from someplace else. A car honks its horn. I didn't notice the guy on my tail. I roll down my window and stick my arm out in the rain to wave him to pass. He zooms by. His car hisses on the wet pavement. I go back to thinking about Evelyn. I open my eyes and find myself on the wrong side of the road. I veer right. I turn on the radio and eat one of Jim's pills. The rain comes down. I hold tight on the wheel.

A car emerges in the eastbound lane. It's moving fast and it begins to weave. It crosses the line, heading straight for me. I swerve. The car, a station wagon, nearly clips me. It roars over a ditch and touches down in a crunch of sheet metal and broken glass. I stomp on the brakes, pop the car in reverse, and back up fast. I jump out of the car. The rain soaks the shirt on my back. I leap over the ditch and run across the field.

"Hey!" I holler. "You okay?"

No response. The car's smashed. It had stopped right-side up and I see at least four people inside. The driver is impaled on the steering wheel. The passenger's head leans against a red-stained cobweb in the glass. I hear moaning in the back. There's two: a man and woman. They're injured and bleeding. I look in the rear. There's no one, just a few valises and a wad of clothes. I carry the woman to my car. I tie a shirt around her arm where it's bleeding. I slip in the mud as I go back for the guy. I get him into my car. I'd passed a town not too far back. I turn the car around and do seventy-five miles per hour in the rain.

It's dark by the time I reach Memphis. The clouds have blown off, and I can see flashes above the horizon as fireworks explode over the river. Boys and young men launch their bottle rockets and light firecrackers throughout the city.

I pull into the driveway. Aunt Norma comes to the door. She tells me to get into some dry clothes. I go upstairs while she makes me supper. I eat. Aunt Norma sits across from me. I tell her what happened, including the car driving off the side of the road. I don't tell her about the morgue.

20

THE SUN BAKES everything it touches. A hot wind brings no relief, and the camels sit with their backs to it. I pull down my burnous to keep the sand out of my eyes as I negotiate with the caravan master to transport me and my goods to a village, a two-day camel ride that will begin after sundown.

The caravan master whistles and two boys appear. They are brothers. They wear breeches and blouses that extend almost to their knees. The two haul the sacks of flour and other items across the sand. Then the boys dig a hole as they sing. It's a language I don't understand. A blind man sits against a wall, and he beats a drum to accompany the children's voices. He smiles in a daze from the kif he's smoking. His teeth are stained yellow and brown.

I ask the boys how they will mark the spot where they bury my goods. The smaller one points to the tarboosh on his head. I laugh and say the wind will blow it away, but the boys just laugh at me.

When the pit is ready, the smaller boy jumps into the hole and he sits with his back against it. His brother drops the sacks onto the boy's lap. He then refills the pit with sand.

The sand covers my goods and the child, until all that remains is the top of the boy's tarboosh. Then the older boy begins again to sing, and the blind man shakes a piece of animal hide on which several bells are sewn.

The tinkling of the bells gets louder. It wakes me; I'm sprawled on the couch. I jump to answer the phone.

"Tommy, this is Claire Williams. I'd like to know what kind of progress you've made finding Helen."

I rub the sleep from my eyes and wish I'd stayed on the couch.

"I've chased a number of leads, even as far away as Nashville, but so far there's been no recent sign of her."

Static fills the silence over the line.

"I'd like you to tell me in person. I let a girlfriend talk me into going shopping this afternoon. She thought it would cheer me up. Meet me in the Balinese Room at the Claridge at three. There will be no one there at that time."

I hang up, then dial Evelyn's number. I tell her I'm sorry I didn't make it back in time, and that I'd meant to call last night, but fell asleep on the couch. She asks me what happened and I tell her about the accident, but not about the two in the front seat.

The smell of coffee drifts in from the kitchen. I follow it in. I need a cup and a cigarette. Aunt Norma turns on the radio.

"You hungry?" she asks.

I nod my head.

"What's the matter?"

"That was Mrs. Williams. I don't have anything good to tell her."

"I don't mean to sound cold, but that comes with the territory. Now if you'd took over that garage from Arthur Groom then you wouldn't have—"

"I don't want to own a garage. I know Arthur made me a decent offer, but the day my name goes over that shop is the day I become a mechanic the rest of my life."

"No, you become the owner of a real business."

"I know what it's like to run a garage. It's not for me."

"What is for you? Trying to find some runaway girl? Making deals to buy back folks' stolen property? You call that making a living?"

"What's wrong with that?"

The toaster pops. Neither of us speaks. She slips the eggs onto a plate and leaves the kitchen.

*　　*　　*

It's a few minutes after two-thirty when I get to the Claridge. I buy a paper and take a seat in the lobby. When it's nearly three, I look over the top of my paper as I hear the elevator bell ding. I see Mrs. Williams and a bellhop step out of the car. I can't help but notice the eye contact between them. He's a good looking kid with blonde hair and lugging bags seems to keep him in shape.

I sit with the paper in front of me as the two stroll past. I think I'm imagining things. But when they give each other a last look, any doubt I have is gone. I haven't finished the article I'm reading, but I can't concentrate after their performance. Still, I wait another few minutes before I get up to meet her.

The Balinese Room is dim. One candle burns in a bamboo lantern on the table where Mrs. Williams primps her hair in a compact mirror. She's right. She knows from experience. The place is empty. Two waiters move like shadows silently setting tables.

"How was your shopping?" I ask as I sit down.

Mrs. Williams makes a cat-like stretch.

"Boring. But I couldn't refuse a girlfriend. Virginia kept badgering me until I agreed to go."

"Must be difficult."

She ignores me and says, "I sent the waiter to get us a pint."

My face gives no expression.

"Whiskey okay with you?"

"That's fine," I say.

Neither of us says anything as the waiter returns. He sets the bottle in its paper bag on the table, along with the change and a receipt. Mrs. Williams tips him. He takes our orders for a setup and leaves.

"So you want to know how my search is going?"

Mrs. Williams withdraws a cigarette from a silver and black enamel case as she says, "Yes, tell me all about it."

I pick up the lighter and light her cigarette. Then I light one of my own.

"There isn't all that much to tell. Maybe if I spoke with her friends?"

She shakes her head as the waiter comes back with our setups. I pour the whiskey into Mrs. Williams's Coca-Cola and some into my empty glass. We have a drink.

"I had a run in with Dale Martins. He was a bigger boy than I expected, but I was able to handle him."

Mrs. Williams sets her chin in the cup of her hand and says, "Do you think he's still seeing Helen?"

"I think he's moved on."

"You're certain?"

"I'm positive."

"Well don't write him off too soon. I know how men are. You mentioned Nashville."

"Yes. A bartender told me he heard Helen say she was going to Nashville to get married."

Mrs. Williams coughs.

"Get married!"

"It was a mistake."

"I'll say. Marriage at her age."

"No. Wrong girl. It wasn't Helen."

"Well that's a relief."

"It was a mistake for her too," I say woodenly. "For the girl I found in Nashville."

Mrs. Williams doesn't ask for an explanation and I don't offer one. I gave my drink a swirl.

"How many times has Helen taken off for more than a day?"

"Five or six."

"What's the longest she's been away?"

She tips the cinders from her cigarette as she says, "No more than a week. Usually two or three days."

"And no phone calls the whole time she's gone?"

"Yes. Helen's cruel that way."

"And it's because she's angry that you got remarried?"

"That's right."

Mrs. Williams looks at the clouds of smoke and says, "Helen used to be the sweetest girl."

"They often are."

"What do you mean?"

"That some things are obvious and some are not."

"What are you getting at?"

I let the whisky slip down my throat.

"That shopping trip you needed to cheer you up."

"What of it?"

"It was a bit more than shopping."

She knocks over her drink. The glass smashes on the floor. A waiter comes and cleans up the mess. She doesn't speak till he's gone.

"Okay, Mr. Rhodeen. What are you trying to say?"

"I got here early. I sat in the lobby and read the paper. You and that bellhop put on quite a show."

"So you saw?" she says in a whisper.

"Of course, but I'm no meddler. You have your reasons. All I want to know is Helen's disappearance on the level? Or am I wasting my time?"

Mrs. Williams face melts and she daubs her eye with a glove.

"I lost everything after Stephen died. I had to go to work. I became Garland's secretary. There was nothing between us before we were married. There's been nothing between us since."

I gulp my drink.

She leans forward and looks into my eyes and says in a child-like voice, "You promise you won't tell Garland?"

"Your husband hired me for one thing. Find the girl he considers his daughter. He didn't hire me to find out if his wife is cheating."

She puts her hand on mine, looks me in the eye and says, "We could get a room."

I yank my hand out from hers. I get up and walk away in disgust. I don't look back.

Crowds of shoppers pass me on the sidewalk as I head for my car. I pull into traffic and think about going to see Evelyn at work. I get halfway across Union and think better of it.

21

THE PHONE RINGS. I jump out of bed. I stub my toe. I hop to the phone and answer it.

"Tommy?"

I favor the other foot as I lean against the wall and say, "Hi Evelyn, how are you?"

"Evelyn? It's June. June Fornsby. Claire Williams's niece. Don't you remember me?"

"Yes. June. Sure. How are you?"

"I'm fine. I'm calling because I have something to show you. I think it might help you find Helen."

"That's great. Thank you. What is it?"

"Come to my house. I'll show them to you. Can you make it before noon?"

June gives me an address in Central Gardens. We hang up. I make breakfast, get dressed, and get ready to go.

I park in front of her house. It isn't the biggest place on Peabody Avenue, but it's nice and it has a porch that wraps around it. A Buick sits in the driveway. I walk past it, go up the steps, and ring the bell. June opens the door. She looks nothing like the girl I met before. June wears red slacks and a white blouse that shows off the shape of her breasts.

"Hi, Tommy. Come in."

She points to the living room and says, "Wait here," as she bounds up the stairs. I go sit on a couch covered in chintz and glance at the magazines on the coffee table. I stand up when she returns. June makes an entrance like a kid; she holds out a small silk bag as if it's some kind of treasure.

"Helen showed me these last month."

She pours a pair of cufflinks onto the coffee table and says, "Yesterday I was at Aunt Claire's. I snuck into Helen's room."

I pick them up. They're squarish with round corners. They look like silver and have four interlocking black rectangular stones that surround a diamond.

"Who gave these to her?"

June smiles.

"Helen told me they belonged to her beau; she wouldn't tell me his name. She said she'd taken them as a souvenir. She made me promise not to tell to Aunt Claire or Uncle Garland."

"That's why you didn't mention them before?"

"Of course. And with Helen gone, I'm not in their house often. I couldn't get them till now."

"They don't know about these?"

"I doubt it."

"Do you think they belonged to Dale Martins?"

June giggles.

"What's so funny?"

"Dale was too much for Helen. She didn't like him pawing at her."

June's no priss like I thought.

"Did you know Helen kept a diary?" I ask.

"Of course. And Helen knew her mother knew. That's why she stopped writing."

I hold out the cufflinks in my palm.

"Can I hang on to these?"

"That's one of the reasons I called you."

"One of the reasons?"

"I'm playing a piano recital Monday. I want you to

come."

"A piano recital?"

"Yes, at the Highland Country Club. Six o'clock."

"I'll be there. Thank you for inviting me. And for the cufflinks."

June smiles and touches my hand. I get up. She walks me to the door.

I drive into town and stop at a jeweler's. The salesman is showing a woman a necklace. He's a fat man sporting a ruby pinky ring, and he nods at me while his customer gazes at herself in the mirror. I go take a look at the watches. When the customer leaves, the man turns to me and says, "How can I help you?"

I show him the cufflinks.

"Can you tell me anything about them?"

"Platinum. The diamonds look around a tenth of a carat. The stones are onyx. I don't recognize the maker's mark."

"Do you know who sells them?"

"Try Brodnax."

I thank him, leave, and walk north. The place is on the ground floor of an office building. I go inside. A man looks from behind a display case as I enter. He gives me the once-over. I set the bag on the counter.

"I was at another shop and they said to try you. I want to show you a pair of cufflinks."

He scratches his ear and says, "This isn't a pawn shop. You think I'll buy them?"

He picks up the phone.

"See? I'm calling the police."

I fish out my P.I. license. He hangs up.

"I just want information."

I roll the cufflinks onto a velvet tray. A dreamy smile spreads over his face. He picks them up to examine. His fingers are long and delicate.

"Very handsome. Platinum, diamond, and black onyx. Where did you get them?"

"From a friend. Do you carry stuff like this?"

He shakes his head. He handles the jewelry as if they arouse him.

"Where in town could I find something like this?"

"You'd have to go to New York or Beverly Hills. Or Paris. They have the French mark for platinum."

"So you haven't seen these here?"

"No."

"Or anyone wearing them?"

"No. I would have remembered that."

"Can you imagine the assistant manager of a movie theater owning these?"

He drops the cufflinks on the tray as if they have the cooties. I pick them up and leave. I go into the phone booth on the corner.

"Trip's Used Cars."

"Hi Evelyn. It's me, Tommy."

"Hi Tommy? How are you?"

"I'm good. Checking out jewelry stores."

"Tommy?"

"It's for the case. Helen's cousin lent me a pair of cufflinks. They belonged to some guy Helen was seeing. Turns out they were made in France. What are you doing Monday night?"

"Are you asking me out?"

"I'm going to take you to a piano recital."

"Sounds fancy."

"It is. And we're still on for Saturday, right?"

"Yes, pick me up at six."

I finish the call and drive home. I get out of my car. I look at the yard. It needs mowing. I go inside, put on some work clothes, and get the mower out of the shed. I work in the sun; the work is mindless and sweaty. I finish and put the mower back. Dust motes swirl about the shed as I push it inside. Mounted on a wall are pairs of pegs. They hold the rake and the other tools that Dan had used to tend to our yard. I grip the sledgehammer and lift it off the floor. The weight feels good in my hands. I bring it up level with my shoulders before I set it down. I close the shed and go in the house. I shower, put on clean clothes, and come downstairs. Aunt Norma's sitting in the parlor, going through old photos. Earlier this morning she'd told me she'd found a box that had been lost for a long time.

"Come here, Tommy."

"Yes, ma'am."

I sit next to her on the couch. She slides the album between our laps.

"You recognize him?"

I look at an old man. His white hair is long and he has a moustache. He wears a frock coat and holds a watch on a chain.

"That's Pawpaw. You and daddy's great grandpa."

"Uh-huh. And who's this?"

"I don't know. Who?"

"That's my aunt, Nell. She died of Bright's disease when she was twenty-six. Bad kidneys. You can see there how she's got edema."

"Is that a parrot on her?" I ask.

"Yeah, that's Polly. She outlived Nell by just ten years. Got bit by a dog. They shot the dog. Buried the parrot."

We turn the pages and pass a collection of relatives, all dead but the two of us viewing them. I point to a girl in ringlets wearing a shift.

"That you?"

"Uh-uh. That's my cousin, Rose. On her sixth birthday. Or maybe it was her seventh? She got a pony named Rowen when she turned seven. There's a photo of him somewhere. I think it fell out. You see anything on the floor?"

She turns the page.

"That's your daddy when he was little."

A small boy in knickers and a lace collar shirt holds a toy boat. His hair is cut straight across his head. His smile is the one I remember seeing when I was little.

"Here's one of him and me at Grandpa's. It must have been just after Christmastime. I can tell because I remember getting that very same dress."

She flips the pages. A smaller version of my parent's wedding photo comes unglued, and Aunt Norma presses it back with the meat of her palm.

"There's you as a baby."

I know the photo; there lies a naked cherub-child with a handful of fingers in its mouth.

*   *   *

I drive back to the Hideaway after supper. Lloyd Mc-Collough and his band are playing. The air hangs like swamp gas. I get a beer and press it against my face. The crowd is different, but I don't learn anything new about Helen. I tilt my head and empty the bottle. My only interest in finding Helen is to get paid. No one seems to like her much and neither do I.

22

AFTER LUNCH, I sit on the edge of my bed and play guitar. I look up. Aunt Norma stands over me. Her face is splotched red and her mouth bunches up like she tastes something awful.

"Did I not ask you to buy a case of jars last week? It's not like you don't live and eat in this house!"

"Okay! I'll get them. I said I would."

"Well get them now. You couldn't smell them strawberries cooking down?"

Aunt Norma storms out the room. I set down my guitar and pick up my keys. It won't take more than twenty minutes.

*   *   *

I come back to the house carrying a case of jars and I set them on the table.

"You got a call," Aunt Norma says as she hands me a note, "but he wouldn't leave a name."

I look at the paper. The message says if I want to find Helen, go to the Holly Tree and ask the bartender. The Holly Tree's a Negro juke joint north of Byhalia. It's an old place. I've driven past it; I've never been inside. But I'm desperate. I halfway dial Harold's number before I hang up. I already owe him a favor.

I look at my watch. I have plenty of time to go and get back before my date with Evelyn. I get in the car and head south. I cross the state line.

A little while into Mississippi, I pass over a creek and slow down. I see the Holly Tree on the left side of the road. It's an old clapboard house. The yard is full of trash and weeds. Tar paper peels up from the roof as if the building suffers from psoriasis. A corrugated awning sags over the front porch. Some beer and RC Cola signs are nailed to the wall.

I pull across the road and park in the dirt next to two old trucks. It's early. The place will be packed by sundown. I step onto the porch. An old yellow dog lies on its side. Its muzzle is thin and gray. The dog opens and closes a film-covered eye as I pass. I pull the screen door open and step inside.

Four colored men play cards. They look at me and shake their heads. I ignore them and walk to the bar. I ask the man behind it for a beer. A cigarette dangles off his lower lip. He stares at me with his hands on the bar, the left of which is scarred from a burn.

"A beer," I repeat.

I put down a quarter. He fetches up a bottle, opens it, and sets it before me. The coin remains untouched.

"Now you didn't come all this way for a beer," he says.

I take a swig. It's cool and it gives me time to think of what to say.

"No. This beer's just a bonus. Someone called me. Said if I ask you, I'll find out about a missing white girl named, Helen."

The man's eyes open wide, his mouth opens wider.

"A missing white girl? Here? Damn. You came a long way for a beer."

"I've traveled further."

He laughs and takes the coin and drops it into a box before joining a couple at the other end of the bar. I drink my beer as I listen to the jukebox. Some men make jokes. They laugh at me, but I don't want any trouble.

The door opens a little later and an old colored man walks in. He wears a worn out pair of overalls. His brogans are in worse shape; the leather is cracked and scuffed from years of use. He takes off his left shoe, looks inside, and sets it on the floor. I get up and walk toward him. His cloudy eyes are rheumy and his earlobes hang long. Several days' grizzle coats his cheeks.

"Dan? Dan Turner?"

The man looks up as he takes a piece of cardboard from his pocket.

"Who?" he says.

"Are you Dan Turner?"

"My name's George Owens."

"Sorry. I got you confused with someone else. Can I buy you a beer?"

"Sheeit. How 'bout you buy me a whiskey."

I get the drinks while George opens a knife and cuts the cardboard to fit his shoe. I come back and set them on the table. I sit across from him. He gestures with his glass, tilts his head, and empties the cup before I so much as taste mine.

"Damn—that goes down better than 'splo. You come around here anytime, kid."

I work on my whisky while George cuts the cardboard for the other shoe.

"So kid, you got a name?"

"Tommy Rhodeen."

The cardboard's too big. He takes it out and says, "So, Mr. Tommy Rhodeen, you come here expectin' to find this Dan Turner?"

"No. I was told I could find a girl I'm looking for. A missing white girl named, Helen."

George sets down the knife. The men playing poker stop betting; their heads turn our way. George scratches his chin and says, "Now, I don't mean to make light of anyone's misfortune. Especially someone who bought me a drink. But that is the funniest thing I've heard in a long time. You comin' in here to find a missin' white girl. Sheeit."

The men chuckle and go back to their game. George trims the cardboard; he puts it in his shoe. I need to go home. But then a woman whispers, "Helen," into my ear and walks away.

George and I watch her. She's tall and wears her hair cut short with spit curls. She sits at a table in the corner and checks her makeup. Her face glows like honey. I nod at George. I get up and approach the woman.

"What do you know about Helen?" I ask as I sit down.

"What's it worth to you, Bright Eyes?"

"Something."

"I thought so. We split it."

"Split what?"

"You think I'm stupid? The reward."

"Right now there ain't nothin' to split."

She places her hand on my wrist and says, "There will be. If I take you to her."

"How do I know you're telling the truth?"

She stands up. The chair legs scrape the floor. I follow her out to the porch. The sound of men's laughter comes through the door.

"Come back," I say.

"If you stop wasting my time."

"Okay, where's Helen?"

"No. You drive. I tell you where to go."

I open the passenger door to my car. She closes it and dangles a key on her finger.

"Nuh-uh, Bright Eyes. We take mine."

It's a Montclair, blue and white. I turn the key in the ignition and ease it onto the road.

She calls out the turns. Soon we bounce along a dirt road. The trees struggle under the kudzu, beyond them is nothing but cotton.

"Next right."

I barely touch the gas pedal as the road becomes two strips of dirt in the weeds. A wave of dust follows the car. I spot a rickety shack. On top lays a rusted tin roof. In front sits a '32 Ford pickup covered with grime. I park by the truck.

"This it?" I ask as we get out of the car. She looks at me like I'm a box of rocks.

"No, Bright Eyes. We here to see my granny. 'Course this it."

She opens the door. The hinges shriek and a bird explodes out of a pine tree. We step inside. Specks of light come through the cracks in the roof, revealing a sea of swirling dust. Three young colored men sit on a bench in front of a warped plank table. They look like brothers and as if they just came off the field. The floor is hard-packed clay.

"That him?" one asks.

"No this here the chief of po-lice. Sheeit, why you askin' stupid questions?"

I smile. I'm not the only one getting her ribbing. I take the opportunity to get in a word.

"So where's Helen?"

The woman places her hand on my chest and says, "What you in so a hurry for, Bright Eyes? I bet you never done ate dark meat?"

The blood flushes my cheeks.

"The sooner I get Helen back, the sooner we split the

reward."

The air rips as something hits my legs. My knees give. I get shoved. I go down. The top of my head caroms off the edge of the bench.

I look up from the floor. The man holds an axe handle; he smacks it twice in his palm as he stares at me. The back of my legs sting and blood oozes from my head. Two of them jerk me to my feet and hold me while another makes a fist. He punches me in the eye. They sit me down hard on the bench. My eye wells up. The top of my head burns. I touch it. My fingers come away dark with blood.

The woman smiles and says, "There's your reward, Bright Eyes." I look at her, my mouth hangs open. She tosses an envelope onto the table as she says, "Oh, and there's this." I pick it up. It has girl's handwriting. Just four words:

To Mom and Dad

"You bring that to her folks."

"You got a funny way of delivering a letter."

"That's to make sure you got the message."

"I got it."

"Good, Bright Eyes. We don't want no confusion."

She turns to the men and says, "Do it like I told you," and leaves. The Mercury eases away. The three men stare at me. One leans against the door jamb with an old shotgun over his knee.

"Go sit in the corner," he grumbles and points with the gun. I move to where he said. A pile of rotting croaker sacks lay on the clay floor. Tacked on the rough timber wall are yellowed advertisements, clipped from magazines, for ladies' girdles and brassieres. I sit down. The blood on my fingers had smudged the back of the envelope. I wipe it off on my pants.

Two of the men roll themselves a cigarette, another fetches up a jelly jar. He unscrews the lid and takes a drink. They pass it back and forth. No one speaks. The light begins to fade. The cut in my scalp clots and my hair sticks to the wound. The door opens, a small colored boy peers into the shack.

"Give it here," the oldest one says.

The boy carries a parcel in his good hand. The other arm ends in a stump. He looks about eight and wears no shoes. He lays the parcel on the table. The man reaches in and produces a coal oil lamp. He strikes a match. The light sputters as the man fiddles with the wick. Satisfied, he reaches again into the bag and takes out more things. They're wrapped in newspaper, and he tosses them to the two other men. They remove the paper, chuck it on the floor, and eat their sandwiches. The boy stares at me while his brothers wolf their food. They finish. One gets up and stretches.

"I got to take a piss," I say.

The man motions with the shotgun and lifts the latch. We go out and, in the failing light, he points the gun to a clump of sumac. I relieve myself there. I turn around and walk back as one of them comes forward, loosening the top of his pants.

They march me to the truck and I climb into the bed. Two of the men and the boy scramble in after me. The man hands them the shotgun. The truck backfires twice and lurches forward. I cling to the letter with one hand and to the side of the truck with the other as we bump over the dirt road. The only sound is the engine. A patch of beggar's lice is stuck along my pant legs. The truck slows to a stop.

"Get out," the one holding the shotgun says.

I stand up and look over the top of the cab. In the gloom, I can make out the gravel road ahead.

"Get out," he repeats. "Now."

I jump to the ground. The one holding the shotgun hops down beside me. He points the way with the barrel.

"You get, now."

I walk toward the gravel road as the man steps onto the running board and climbs into the cab. I hear the gears shift behind me. The pickup rakes me with its headlights, then passes. It makes a left at the crossroads. The truck's taillight vanishes in a veil of carbon monoxide and dust. I keep going. At the road, I turn right. It's at least a four mile walk until I reach the highway, and from there I can try to thumb a ride.

The air is muggy and the moon has yet to rise. There's no light in any direction save for the stars and the blinking of a radio tower far off in the distance. My scalp and eye ache. I walk with my hands out in front of me. Bats hunt mosquitos; their dark shapes fly herky-jerky across the deep night sky.

Something lands on my shoulder. I brush it to the ground. I squat and in the starlight make out a praying mantis before it takes off into the night. I trudge on. Further down the way some animal slips silently into the brush. I stop walking. I listen.

I hear the purr of an engine. Then headlights arc across the road as a car comes around the bend. Its wheels crunch the gravel. I flag it down. The driver stops. An old man leans out the window and says, "What the hell you doing out here?"

"I got lost," I tell him.

"Well get in."

The old man looks at me under the dome light. His eyes open wide.

"Whoa, son, let me take you to a doctor."

"No, I just need to get home."

"Where's that?"

"Memphis. Which way you going?"

"Up about Olive Branch."

"Can you drop me off a little past Byhalia? My car's there."

He sets the car into drive. The dashboard lights his face a fiery red. I study the way his mouth keeps working as if he's chewing on something that isn't there.

"My name's Henry, what's yours?"

"Tommy."

"What you fight over, Tommy?" he asks as he drives.

"I was looking for a girl."

"Her brothers give you that?"

"No. She run off. I'm trying to find her for her folks."

"Uh-huh."

Henry slows down to skirt some dips, then he turns his head.

"I used to be a scrapper when I was 'bout your age. Fighting and drinking. Wife said she'd leave if I didn't straighten out. She'd a done it too."

"I expect she would."

"Dang right she would. I settled down. Been married forty-seven years. Had nary a drop since."

The old man's mouth goes back to making chewing motions. I tap the envelope on my knee. He turns north at the highway and tells me about some of the stuff he got into when he was young. Soon we come up to the Holly Tree.

"Here's where I get off."

Henry stops the car and shakes his head.

"Here? You looking to get even or worse?"

"Neither. That's my car over there."

"Want me to wait till you get in?"

"No, I'll be okay."

I thank him and step out. A blend of music and laughter comes out of the Holly Tree as I head for my car. The old man idles the engine while I walk. I hold up my keys for him to see. I get in, toss the envelope on the seat, and start the motor. I flip on the headlights. Henry waves and takes off. I light a cigarette and look down at the envelope. The sound of something breaking comes from inside the juke joint. Two men are thrown out. They shout curses and charge back inside. Bottles smash and a woman screams. I get onto the road.

It's almost eleven when I pull up in front of Evelyn's house. The porch light's on and so is a light or two inside. I pick up the envelope and get out. A cat darts between my legs as I knock on the door.

The sound of footsteps answers from the other side.

"Who is it?"

"Evelyn, it's me. Tommy."

"Don't you think you're a little late?"

"I'm sorry, Evelyn. It was, uh... I got beat up."

She opens the door, looks at me, and gasps.

"Tommy, what happened?"

She brings me in, and fetches some ice and a washcloth. I hear feet come down the stairs. Trip stands in his pajamas and says, "What the heck happened to you?"

"I got set up."

Evelyn inspects my head. Her momma looks from the stairs and gathers her robe.

"Where did this happen?" Evelyn asks.

"Someone left a message telling me to go to this place. They said I'd find Helen."

"You found something all right," she replies.

I hold up the letter. She sets it on the table and goes

back to nursing my head.

Trip picks it up and says, "They gave you that and beat you up?"

"Yeah, but the other way around. They hit me first."

Evelyn lifts the ice pack to look.

"You work with such nice people."

She holds the ice back to my head; I set my hand on top of hers.

23

I WASH MY FACE and shave. In the mirror I see the beginnings of a black eye. My legs itch from some chigger bites I must have got last night. I get dressed and go downstairs. Aunt Norma looks at me as I sit at the table.

"You start boxing again?"

I don't say anything. She sets down a plate of eggs and pours me a cup of coffee.

"I think this job's over."

"Well, I'm glad to hear that. Where did you find her?"

"I didn't. She wrote a letter. I'll bring it to the Williamses after they get home from church."

Aunt Norma nods and lights a cigarette. I can tell she's thinking about bringing up Arthur Groom and his garage. I finish my breakfast and do the dishes.

*   *   *

The butler opens the door. He ignores my eye and says, "Hello, Mr. Tommy. How can I help you?"

"I have something for Mr. and Mrs. Williams."

"None of them's home. Was they expecting you?"

"No. Where are they?"

"At his brother's. At Mr. Edward's."

He notices the envelope in my hand.

"Mr. Tommy, you could leave that letter with me. I'll see Mr. Garland gets it."

"I have to deliver it. Where does Edward live?"

He gives me an address in Chickasaw Gardens. I drive over. A maid answers the door.

"Yes, sir, may I help you?"

"I'm here to see Mr. and Mrs. Garland Williams. Their butler told me they're here."

"Whom may I ask is calling?"

"Tommy. Tommy Rhodeen."

I wait in the foyer. It's sunny. A bouquet of flowers stands on a narrow table, over which a mirror hangs on the wall. I peek at my eye. I see the maid walk toward me in the reflection.

"They just finished eating. Please come this way," she says.

I follow her though a fancy living room and out a pair of double doors. She leads me onto the patio. She stops and I continue on to where they are seated with Edward and his wife. They're drinking tea under a large umbrella that shades the glass-covered table. The silver set includes a teapot, creamer, and sugar bowl.

Garland Williams sets down his cup as I approach.

"Why, Mr. Rhodeen, does this mean you have information about Helen? And what may I ask has happened to your eye?"

"I have a letter I think is from Helen," I say as I hand him the envelope. I make up a story about running into a door, but no one seems to be listening.

Garland reads the letter with his wife, while Edward introduces me to his.

"Margaret, this is Tommy Rhodeen. He's the one who's been searching for Helen."

She offers me her hand and winces at my bruise. I tell her I'm pleased to meet her, but neither of us makes any more small talk as Garland and Claire read the letter. I wait till they've read it through several times.

"Does the handwriting look like Helen's?" I ask.

Mrs. Williams's face pales.

"Yes. Yes. I'm afraid it does."

"And the message?"

Her face crushes and she starts to cry.

"I don't understand."

Mr. Williams pats his wife's hand. He gets up with the letter and takes Edward and me aside. His large hand rests on the back of my shoulder; he pushes me forward as he leads us to the other side of the pool. He then hands the letter to his brother and me. We read it together.

It's not what I expected. Helen asked her parents to forgive her. She wrote that she didn't want to embarrass them, and that she didn't know how to tell them, and that she promised she could come home in February, and not to worry, and that she was sorry. It was signed Helen.

I was about to speak when Garland raises a hand.

"It means Helen's with child," he says flatly.

We walk back to the table. Garland rejoins his wife, slides the letter back into the envelope, and puts it into his pocket. Edward looks at me and bites his lip.

Garland holds his wife's hand and says to me, "I think this ends our business."

"I guess it does," I say. "I'm sorry how it turned out."

"We appreciate what you've done. And while it was not the result we'd hoped for, you've brought us peace of mind. Come by my office tomorrow and I'll write you a check."

"Mr. Williams, I didn't bring Helen home."

"Nonsense. You did your job and as I told you, you brought us peace of mind. Besides, it looks like you worked hard."

Mrs. Williams blows her nose and says, "I bet it was

that Dale Martins." She sits forward and grips the edge of the table.

I face her and say, "I understand you're angry, but I spoke with Dale. I don't think it's him."

Edward puts his hand on my elbow.

"You don't really know that," he says. "But that's not what's important now. We know why Helen left and when she can come home. Tommy, you will keep this confidential."

"Of course I will."

"Good," Garland says. "Come to my office."

He gives me the address. I thank him and turn to his wife. I want to say more, but I've said all I can. She looks like she needs to hurt someone, and if I say another word it could be me.

The maid sees me to the door. The air feels fresh as I walk to my car. I'm free of looking for Helen, and soon I'll have another five hundred dollars to show for it. I'm glad to get my old life back, even if that means doing more recovery work. But now I want to take Evelyn to the best place in town and to get that new guitar.

24

THE RECEPTIONIST sits opposite the door. She looks at me as I come in and asks if I have an appointment.

"Yes," I tell her. "Mr. Williams is expecting me."

"Garland or Edward?"

"Garland."

"And your name is?"

"Tommy Rhodeen."

She smiles.

"Yes, Mr. Williams told me you'd be coming. He's in a meeting. Please be seated."

I settle onto the leather couch and look through the magazines on the coffee table. A half hour later, the inner door opens and the sound of laughter bursts into the room. Garland leads three men past me; he doesn't acknowledge I'm there. The three continue out the door and into the hall.

Garland closes the door after they leave, turns and says, "Tommy, thank you for coming." I get up, he shakes my hand, and we go into his office. Photographs of Garland standing next to state and local politicians hang near the entrance. A wall is shelved with law books, and another is devoted to trophies. I see the head of the grizzly he killed; the one I'd seen in that photo in his cabin. Also mounted is the head of an elk and a pronghorn buck. His huge desk is uncluttered. He sits behind it and indicates the chair on the other side.

"Son," he says, "how long have you been doing this

sort of work?"

"Nearly a year, sir."

"Does it pay well?"

"Some days better than others. But it beats working on cars."

"Military?"

"Yes, with the Third Infantry Division in West Germany. I was a mechanic on APCs. Armored personnel carriers."

"So you didn't see any action?"

"That's correct."

"And when you got home?"

"I swapped out repairing tanks for repairing cars."

"And how was that different?"

"If I talked back to the sergeant, I'd have pulled extra duty. But I wasn't going to take guff from a garage owner who isn't a better mechanic than me."

"Meaning?"

"I quit two times and was fired once."

"Then what did you do?"

"Kept working on motors, sir. In the driveway."

Mr. Williams places his hands in front of him.

"I hear you got into your current line of business because you got Judge Buchanan back his dog."

I laugh as I say, "Well, that bit of luck helped fix me up with a private investigator license. But I'd already been recovering stolen property for two months."

He smiles and leans back in his chair.

"Yes, you can never underestimate the power of good luck. But the first rule of political favors is everything is personal. Political favors. That's how things get done."

The words hit me like a rock. I'd always felt getting my P.I. license was me getting an even break. But now it didn't feel so honest and I wished I'd never bragged about it. I look up. Mr. Williams had asked me another question. He could tell I hadn't heard.

"So you still work on cars?"

"Sometimes. That and play music."

"Yes, that's right. I think I told you, you're playing that rock and roll is why I hired you. Seemed like the right choice as far as Helen."

He opens a checkbook and takes the cap off a pen.

"We're glad your investigation convinced Helen to write us that letter. Not knowing whether she was living or dead, that was the most difficult."

He hands me the check and says, "Paid in full."

I look at the check. It would take a whole lot of stolen property cases to make that kind of money.

"That's very generous, sir. But I didn't bring your daughter home."

"She will come home in time."

"May I ask you a question, sir?"

"Certainly."

"Do you think Dale Martins is…?"

"Is the father?"

I nod my head.

"I don't know."

He swivels in his chair. I think our conversation has ended. Then he spins around, picks a Bible off his desk, and flips through the pages.

"Let me read you something. 'He that uttereth a slander is a fool.' Proverbs 10:18."

It's a side of him I didn't expect. I put out my hand.

"May I, sir?"

He hands me the Bible. I find the page.

"For if ye forgive men their trespasses, your heavenly Father will also forgive you."

Mr. Williams smiles and says, "Keep reading."

"But if ye forgive not men their trespasses, neither will your Father forgive your trespasses."

He leans forward in his chair and chuckles.

"Matthew, right? There's a whole lot of forgiveness in there. But to get back to your question. When I find out who's responsible, Dale Martins or whomever, I will not be so full of forgiveness."

He gets up and says, "Walk with me."

We cross his office to the corner, where the windows come together. Garland moves his big body like a bear. He rises as he looks out the windows, over the river and to the northern part of the city below. It's as if there's something out there he can smell. Something he wants and can get.

"What do you see?" Mr. Williams asks.

I wasn't sure. I know he's referring to more than just the city. He turns his head slowly, as if he's taking in the entire view that unfolds beneath us.

"Change and opportunity. There are great changes coming to this country and to this city. And a smart man, a decisive man who has his eyes wide open to change, can make a great fortune."

I'm not used to this kind of speaking and I find myself nodding my head and saying, "You're right, sir."

He turns to me. He rests his massive hand on my shoulder and leads me back to his desk.

"Speaking of eyes what happened to yours?"

"Bit of a sucker punch. It wouldn't have happened in a fair fight."

The intercom squawks. He pushes the lever with one of his chunky fingers.

"What is it, Alice?"

"Mr. Smith is here."

He pushes it again.

"Tell him to wait. Mr. Rhodeen will be leaving us shortly."

He extends his arm and says, "We'll talk again soon, Tommy."

As we shake hands, mine disappears in his. He walks me to the door. In the lobby is a man. He sits in a chair and holds a long cardboard tube, the kind used to store maps and drawings. I leave.

25

I GO CASH THE CHECK. The bank manager seems to remember me, but he says he still needs to call before he can take it. I don't care as long as the check is good. I get the cash, drive home, and make dinner reservations to surprise Evelyn after June's recital.

At four fifteen, I shave and slip into a clean shirt and stuff my feet into a fresh pair of socks. I put on my suit and get into the car. There's no traffic and I arrive at Trip's car lot a few minutes after five. Evelyn wears a mint green dress and matching shoes. She looks great. I tell her it's hard to drive and keep my eyes on the road with her sitting next to me.

We drive through the country club gates. We're early, so we look around at the golf course and at the low hills and at the stands of oak, birch, and sugarberry. The sunlight falls across her hair. I touch it as I remove a leaf. I pretend to hit a golf ball; it's a hole-in-one. We hold hands.

A colored woman in a nurse's uniform pushes an old man in a wheelchair along the cement path. She stops and sets the brake before tucking in the blanket that had slipped from his chest. He smiles at us as we pass.

"I wanted to be a nurse when I was eight or nine," Evelyn says. "I'd seen a newsreel. It was during the war. They were army nurses. The patients were soldiers. The women looked strong and capable."

"Why didn't you?"

"Become a nurse? My brother and daddy were going to open a new car dealership when he came home. But that changed when Billy died. I'd already been working for my daddy after school. I just kept on working there. I never got to go to nursing school."

Evelyn puts her hand on my waist and I put mine around hers as we head toward the clubhouse.

"Sometimes I think about it. Assisting the surgeons. Not that I don't like managing the car lot. And daddy taught me the business. He thought everything changed when Billy died. And of course it had. But he believes in me and in a few years we may open a new car dealership.

"I'd be lying if I said I'm not happy the way things turned out. I don't mean what happened to Billy. I mean working in the car business. I never had a choice. I'm not complaining, mind you, and if I had a choice I'd wish Billy was alive. That has nothing to do with whether I got to become a nurse or not. I guess it's just realizing that you need to make the best of things, otherwise life can be pretty grim."

Evelyn smiles as we climb the stairs. A man in a green jacket stands by the door.

"Are you members?"

"No, we're guests of June Fornsby." I say. "The name's Rhodeen."

The man looks at a sheet of paper on a clipboard.

"Rhodeen, Thomas. No mention of additional guests."

I let go of Evelyn's hand.

"Well that's a mistake."

The man grins and says, "I go by what's on the list."

"You may have a job, but that don't give you cause to act like this."

I take a step toward him. If I can't make him see reason, I'm ready to shove that list down his throat. I set my weight on my back foot as I hear someone call my name. I follow the sound of the voice; Edward Williams stands at the top of the stairs as if he's on a stage.

"Why, Mr. Rhodeen, I didn't know you were coming."

"June invited me."

"Well, that's wonderful."

"But there's been a mix up. I'm listed as June's guest, but there's nothing about my date."

Edward notices Evelyn. He looks her up and down before turning to the man with the list.

"Summers. Mr. Rhodeen and his date are welcome."

"Yes, Mr. Williams."

The man nods and steps out of our way. We enter the hall. Edward chatters how much he looks forward to June's performance. He then waves goodbye as he joins his wife. We get to our seats. Neither Garland nor Claire seems to be in the audience.

The room begins to applaud as June takes the stage. She sits at the piano. The people stop talking. Someone coughs and finally the room is quiet.

June plays Beethoven's *Moonlight Sonata;* at least that's what it says in the program. The music starts slowly. Then the pace picks up, almost skipping along. It sure wasn't Jerry Lee Lewis, but she plays in a way you'd never expect from a girl. Not that this is the kind of music I normally listen to, but I know talent when I hear it.

The music stops. Evelyn and I applaud. June curtsies and disappears into the wings. Other people don't seem so impressed, and I hear talk of everything but the music. We leave the auditorium and someone calls my name. I turn. There's June. Her eyes are bright.

"Tommy! I'm so glad you came."

"June, you were wonderful. Honestly, I can't believe it."

I introduce Evelyn to June. June rushes off without a word. Evelyn takes hold of my hand and says, "Now I know why I wasn't on the list." I squeeze her hand. We laugh as we walk to my car.

I don't tell Evelyn where we're going. We drive out the gates of the country club. I aim the car south and soon pull up in front of the Embers. I hold open the door and we walk inside.

"Rhodeen, party of two," I say to the host. "We have a reservation."

He skims his finger down the page and says, "Yes, sir, right this way." The host leads us past an indoor waterfall that runs down the rocks set into the wall. He then takes us to our table.

"What do you think?" I ask.

"It's beautiful. I've never been to a place like this."

We open our menus and decide what to have. The waiter comes. I order.

"My date will start with the gulf shrimp cocktail and then have the filet mignon. I'll begin with the charbroiled shrimp and then the T-bone."

"Very good," the waiter says. "Medium rare?"

I look at Evelyn and she gives me a quick nod.

"Yes, medium rare."

The waiter takes our menus and leaves us alone. I reach over and hold Evelyn's hand. She makes me feel glad. Our food arrives and we have a wonderful time.

We get back in my car after supper. I think of a place we can park. *Heartbreak Hotel* comes on the radio. Evelyn asks if I know Elvis. I do. He used to watch me and my friends box when we trained for the Golden Gloves.

"Sure, I know him," I say.

"You like him?"

"Elvis? Well a lot of guys don't. But how can a musician not like Elvis?"

"What do you mean?"

"A lot of guys... They get bent out of shape when they see Elvis. Like that fistfight he got into at that service station."

"Why is that?"

"Because the way he's around girls. The way they all react to him. All that screaming and fussing."

"That's a silly reason not to like him."

"That's the way it is."

"And that's how you feel?"

My ears get hot.

"Elvis is a great performer," I say.

"So you're jealous of him, too."

"Jealous? Me?"

"You're saying you're not?"

I snap off the radio. Any chance to park has gone. Evelyn doesn't say anything. I don't say anything. I drive. I stop the car in front of her house. She looks at me and tries to smile.

"I'm sorry I kidded you."

"That's okay," I lie.

"It was a great evening. The recital, the restaurant. I'm sorry I made a mess of it."

I open the passenger door. Evelyn steps out and I walk her up to the porch. She takes my hand and says, "Tommy, we got to know each other so fast and I got scared. I kind of acted silly. I'm sorry."

"I understand."

She gives me a kiss on the cheek, opens the door, and goes inside. I get back in my car and go to a place to shoot pool. Games are underway on two of the tables. I watch with my back against the wall.

"Eight ball?"

The guy wears his hair in a D.A. and has on a pair of dungarees and an open collar sport shirt in royal blue.

"Buck a game?" I reply.

He nods. We each set a dollar under the ashtray. We flip; he brakes and takes solids. He sinks five balls and misses. I start dropping stripes into the pockets.

"Twelve in the side."

I bank it off the cushion; it rolls in. Soon I have two balls left before I can go for the eight. I put the fourteen away. That leaves me with the ten. Earlier it stopped on the edge of a pocket. I figure out the angles. I hit it. I hit it too hard. The ten drops into the hole. The cue ball goes in right behind. The guy takes back the game. He taps in the eight, picks up the two bucks and says, "Rematch?"

I open my wallet. I feel someone's standing next to me. I turn around. He asks if I'm Tommy Rhodeen. The guy looks familiar. Crew cut, towheaded, he wears a short sleeve plaid shirt and chinos.

"Yeah, that's me."

"You still looking for that Helen Williams?"

"Not anymore. Why?"

"I drive a truck for a laundry service. I think I saw her the other day."

"Let's talk outside."

The guy with the D.A. waves the money and says, "You want a rematch or not?"

I shake my head. Crew cut and I walk out.

"This place on your route, is it some kind of home for unwed mothers?"

"Yeah. So you know?"

"Not where, but I'm hip to the idea."

"So you're not in the market for information?"

"Nope. If you found me a few days earlier it'd be another story."

26

I DRIVE to Frank's Music. I get there a little bit after he opens. He's demonstrating an accordion to a kid and his mother when I walk in. I look around. They leave five minutes later without buying anything. Frank crosses his arms. I spread four hundred-dollar bills on the counter.

"I told you I wasn't wasting your time."

Frank picks up the money and smiles.

"Let me get you your guitar."

He takes the orange Gretsch 6120 off the wall. I plug it into the amplifier I used before. It sounds big and it makes everything I went through worthwhile.

"How much for the Champ?" I ask.

"Fifty bucks and it's yours. And I'll throw in the cord and two sets of strings."

"Deal."

I drive home. I finally have a real guitar. I bring it into my room and wash up. I plug the guitar into the amp and turn on the power. The phone rings. I answer.

"Mr. Rhodeen, this is Alice. Mr. Williams's secretary."

"Yes?"

"Mr. Williams would like you to have lunch with him and Edward today."

"That sounds fine."

"They'll meet you at Ken's Place. Across from the Peabody. Noon okay with you?"

"Please tell Mr. Williams I'll be there."

There's just enough time to change before I have to

get back in the car. I put my guitar in its case.

I walk in the door at Ken's and tell the maître d' I'm meeting the Williamses. He points the way using his arm. Then someone calls my name. Edward comes toward me.

"I had to take a phone call," he says. As we walk, I tell Edward how much I enjoyed June's recital, and I ask if he has any children.

"No, I'm afraid we've been unable to."

He says it as if he's commenting on the weather; I shouldn't have asked. Edward waves at his brother.

"Look who I found."

Garland gets up and shakes my hand. He has me sit between them. I sit. He pours me a drink. I drink.

"Tommy," Garland says. "Edward and I have been talking about you and we think you could be a great help to us."

"How can I do that?"

"By becoming one of those rock and roll performers," he replies.

I think they're joking. I'm about to say so and Garland explains their proposal.

"Tommy, I've done a lot for this city working behind the scenes. It's a noble pursuit that I've dedicated my life to. I ran for mayor once. Against Jim Pleasants, E.H. Crump's man. That was 1947 and I lost. In retrospect, I probably would have even if Crump hadn't put his weight behind Pleasants. As you can see, I was not blessed with a face for politics. But Edward is and the times most certainly are changing."

The waiter appears; we order lunch. Then Edward makes his point.

"Tommy, we've made inroads with every community within Memphis. But since Crump died, no single person has taken citywide control of the elections. So we must do everything we can to get enough votes."

I look at the brothers.

"And how does me becoming a rock 'n' roll performer help you get elected?"

Edward smiles and places his hands on the table.

"Young voters today have different interests than their parents."

"And we need to do something special to appeal to them," Garland adds.

All I ever wanted was to become a professional musician. They think it's easy.

"You think I can be a rock 'n' roll star, just like that?"

The two brothers laugh.

"Exactly," says Garland as he sets down his glass. "Sam Phillips needs money. The manufacturing and shipping costs are exhausting the capital he needs to promote his recording artists, and so we offered to make a sizable investment in Sun Records."

I shake my head.

"Sam's heard me, he wasn't impressed. Neither was Dewey."

"That was then," says Garland. "For a little upfront money, our radio station owner friends will see to it that your new records go into... What is that phrase?"

"Heavy rotation," Edward says.

"Yes. Heavy rotation," Garland repeats and puts his cigarette in his mouth.

"I don't know."

I take a drink and frown. Edward notices.

"We'll get you a manager," he says. "It'll all be professional."

He leans back in his chair.

"After your hit, you'll record a campaign song we can get on the air and perform at my rallies."

I feel sick. Garland puts his hand on my arm.

"Tommy, you will have done Memphis a great service by helping Edward get elected mayor. As a reform candidate concerned for the common man, Edward will do great things that will help get our city back on track. I'm thinking not just now, but into the next decade and beyond."

The waiter arrives with our steaks. I use the diversion to think and still don't like the idea.

"Tommy," says Edward, "I see you lack confidence, but I promise with our backing you will become a great success."

I can't eat. My steak has too much butter. It tastes too rich, and it only adds to my queasiness.

"Thank you. I appreciate what you and Garland want to do for me. And I—"

Garland holds up his fork.

"Then it's settled."

27

TWO DAYS later, I get the phone call.

"Hello, Tommy, this is Joe Mellon."

I know his name and his voice. Joe's a popular radio announcer and he's managed several singers.

"Hello, Joe. I guess the Williams brothers spoke with you."

"Indeed, they have. I've heard great things about you."

I don't want to shill for a politician, but I'm excited that someone's interested in my career, even if he's getting paid to.

"What are we going to do?" I ask.

"Make a lot of records for starters."

"I could go for that."

"Good! Meet me over at Taylor's. We'll have us some coffee and a slice of cake, and we'll plan your rise to fame and fortune. How's four this afternoon?"

"That'll be great."

I hang up, holler, and run to the kitchen. I give Aunt Norma a kiss. She thinks I lost my mind. I flip through the city directory. I dial. The phone rings seven times. I'm ready to hang up. Someone answers. They drop the phone. I hear it bang against the wall. There's muffled noises, then someone speaks:

"Hello."

"Walter! "This is Tommy Rhodeen. How are you?"

"Who?"

"Tommy Rhodeen. You played on my recording."

"Tommy… Rhodeen… Yeah, I remember you. How you doin'?"

"Great. I just got off the phone with Joe Mellon. He's going to be my manager and we're going to make a bunch of rock 'n' roll records. I want you to play on them."

There's a pause. I'm about to ask if he's still there. Then Walter speaks:

"That sounds cool, but I don't think Joe will go for it."

"We're going to meet this afternoon."

"You let me know what he says."

"Okay."

"You do that. Bye now."

I get ready for my meeting. I jump in the car and go.

Joe Mellon's reading the paper when I walk into Taylor's.

"Mr. Mellon?" I say.

"Tommy, sit down."

We shake hands. He tells me to call him Joe. He's about thirty-five and his clothes look like they come from Lansky's. He turns around and tells the waitress to bring two slices of chocolate cake and another cup of coffee.

"I'm glad you're here, Tommy. You impressed your backers and I enjoy breaking in new talent. I'm excited we're gonna be working together."

"That's nice. I mean I'm excited, too."

The waitress brings us our cake. She tops off Joe's cup and fills mine. Joe waits till she leaves; then he lowers his voice.

"I checked you out. I heard you boxed so I called Dorsey. He says you're a good guy. Maybe a bit of a goof. But you could have been a Golden Gloves if you tried."

Joe pushes his cake aside.

"No matter what the Williamses told you, this is going to be hard work. There's things we can do for you, but you gotta hold up on your end."

I set down my coffee and take a breath.

"I was a teenager then. But I've been in the army and I'm different from that kid who didn't train."

"That's all I want to know." He takes a bite of cake and says, "Tommy, you're an unknown. So we need to figure how to get you over with the kids. I want to hear you sing after we finish here, so we can work on your style."

I nod my head. Joe keeps talking:

"I'm thinking the A-side of your record should be a rock 'n' roll version of a song that's done well on either the country and western or the rhythm and blues charts. I've lined up a songwriter to do an original for the B-side."

"I write too."

Joe smiles.

"I won't make any promises," he says.

"That's fair enough."

"Now for a backup band, I have just the right guys."

"I want Walter Otis to play lead guitar."

Joe presses his back against the seat and drops his fork.

"Walter Otis? He's a Negro."

"Sure he is. And the best guitar player in town."

"Now how do you know of Walter?"

"I had another guy lined up to play on my demo, but he couldn't make it. Walter just finished a session, and Sam asked if I didn't mind playing with a colored. Well of course not, considering it was a colored man who taught me guitar in the first place. So Walter played and did a better job than that other guy could've."

Joe closes his eyes for a moment.

"Walter's a fine guitar player. Maybe one of the best.

But your backers want a band that can play in public. Not just make a record. Walter Otis? That's going to be a problem."

"Walter played on my first recording and I told him he always will."

"And how many sessions have you recorded?"

"Just that one."

"You need to let me do my job."

I light a cigarette. The door opens; someone walks toward the table and speaks:

"Hey, Joe."

"Johnny! It's great to see you. Johnny, this is Tommy Rhodeen. Tommy, this is Johnny Cash."

I had stood up as soon as I heard his voice. I shake his hand.

"I'm pleased to meet you Mr. Cash. Congratulations on getting on the Grand Ole Opry."

Johnny smiles.

"Well, thank you. Are you a musician?"

"I aim to be."

"I'm going to manage this boy and make something of him."

"I bet you will."

"You want to sit down?" Joe asks.

"Can't. I gotta go pick up some sandwiches for the road. Good luck to you, Tommy."

He walks to the counter. Johnny Cash. For the first time I feel like I'm in the music business. I take another bite of cake. We finish and walk to the studio next door.

Marion gets up from her desk as we come inside. She tells us Sam is out, which is fine since I don't want him to hear me yet. Joe waves at Roland. We see him through the window setting up in the studio.

We go in. Joe introduces us. I've heard him play on

several records. Now he's going to play on mine. There's three acoustic guitars out; Roland asks me which one I want to play. I pick a Gibson. I adjust the strap and check the tuning. Roland plugs in his guitar and asks me what songs I know.

"How about *Rock with Me Baby*?" I say.

He plays the opening riff. I sing it like how Billy Lee Riley did it. As soon as the last note ends, I strum the opening chords to *Trouble Bound*. Roland winks at Joe and follows me in. I give that bluesy song all the sadness it can hold. Those two songs help show my range. Not that I can claim the idea's mine; they're the A- and B-sides of a Billy Lee Riley single that Roland played on.

"That's great," Joe says. "How about another up-tempo one?"

"Okay, how about *Tear It Up*?"

"Tear it what?" Roland says deadpan.

"You know… The Rock 'n Roll Trio song."

Roland laughs and launches into the song. We finish and he asks if I knew *Slow Down*. I nod and say, "The Jack Earls song? Sure."

"Yeah, that's the one."

We play some more. Marcus sits in on bass. Then Sam pops in and likes what he hears.

28

THE THREE OF US get together the next day. Joe brings a bunch of records. We're looking for a song for us to record. Nothing clicks until Joe puts on the B-side of a Ruth Brown single. *Mend Your Ways* has a rhythm and blues beat and gutsy lyrics that rhyme *You better mend your ways* with *Or I'm gonna end your days*. It's perfect. We work out the chords. We get it going twice as fast as the Ruth Brown version. Sam comes in. We play it again. He turns to me and says, "You got a girlfriend?"

"I'd been seeing this one but—"

"She cheat on you?"

"No. Evelyn and I. We got into a little argument."

"Well play it again. But this time imagine your Evelyn's the girl in the song."

I do my best. It must have worked because after we finish Sam says, "So what y'all thinking for the B-side?" I'm going to suggest one of mine, but Joe chimes in.

"Clement wrote a new song. He showed it to Roland last night. It's called *Two More to Go*."

Sam nods his head and says, "Let's hear it."

Roland sets a sheet of paper on the table. I look at the words while he plays.

After it ends I say, "Here's one of mine," and I play the intro to *Summertime Sue*.

Sam cuts me off after a bit.

"That's great, Tommy," he says. "We'll try it too, but learn Jack's song first. He's got some others that Cash is gonna record."

Roland shows me the chords and we go through it a bunch of times, but I have to keep looking at the paper to get all the words. In truth, it isn't a bad song. I just want to record one of mine.

We then go next door to get something to eat. Afterward, the fellas agree to learn *Summertime Sue*. I show them the song. I feel great.

I turn to Roland as we put away the equipment and tell him, "Let's practice over the weekend. I'd hate to come in Monday and start all over."

"You'll do fine, Tommy. You don't want to sound too rehearsed. It kills the song."

We say goodbye, and I get in my car. I didn't feel like going home so I stop for a beer. Someone calls my name. I turn around and see Trip Rudder heading for me.

"Hey, Tommy, how are you?"

I don't know what Evelyn told him.

"I'm good. I'm doing a single for Sun Records."

Trip slaps my back and says, "Sun Records! That's fantastic! Lot of great guys still there. Johnny Cash. Jerry Lee Lewis. Now you!"

I grin.

"Well I'm not one of them. Yet."

"Hey, you ever find that T-Bird, or that girl you were looking for?"

"No, but Garland Williams was okay with that letter."

Trip gestures with his thumb and says, "Come on back here. I got a table."

We sit down.

"How's business?" I ask.

"Fine. Everyone needs a car. So you're gonna be on Sun Records. Wow, that's something."

"Yeah, I'm excited. Music. That's what I want to do."

"That's what I heard."

Trip offers me a cigarette. We each light up. As he exhales he says, "So Garland Williams, you were working for him?"

"Yeah, you know him?"

"Know of him."

"Meaning?"

"I got a cousin who works at the county seat. He's heard Garland's into some unusual land deals."

"Unusual? You mean not usual or illegal?"

Trip laughs.

"Depends on which way the wind's blowing," he says.

I gulp my beer. Trip tells me what he knows.

"You know, when Garland ran for mayor; when was it? About ten years ago. There were some rumors. Nothing ever came of them when he pulled out of the race."

"What? I thought he lost."

"No. He quit and threw his support for Pleasants. But he didn't get anything in return. Like superintendent of something or other. I think he got a heavy lid set down on some files. Now I hear his brother, Edward, is gonna run."

I shake my head.

"Something the matter?"

"No. Just thinking about this recording session."

"Right. Is this your first time doing a record?"

"I did a small one once. An acetate. Demo really. This is different. More professional. That one doesn't count."

"I'd like to hear this new one. You'll get me a copy?"

"Sure I will."

"You'll autograph it for me?"

I laugh. So does Trip. I buy us another round.

29

I LEAN OVER the toilet, my hands clench the seat. My guts finally stop. Strings of vomit hang from my mouth and chin. I spit. I flush. I shuffle to the sink. I rinse my mouth and wash my face. The door opens. I see Joe in the mirror.

"You all right?"

I sway a bit.

"Uh. Yeah. I'll be okay."

He hands me a towel and leaves. I hear the guys play my song. I rinse my mouth again, walk back into the studio, and push a grin across my face.

"Sorry about that, fellas."

Roland smiles and says, "You ain't the first guy to lose his lunch in there."

I ask him for an E and tune my guitar.

"I'll get it right this time," I say.

We play *Two More to Go* for the twelfth time. I don't flub the words. I get through it, but not as good as on *Mend Your Ways*. On that one I only needed two takes.

"Let's try again," Sam says.

We do. It doesn't sound right. We switch back to *Summertime Sue*.

Roland shakes his head after several more takes. Sam comes out of the control room and says, "Well, we got us an A-side."

I look at the floor. Joe taps me on the shoulder.

"We'll come back; we'll get that other song."

"I'm sorry about today," I say.

Joe tells me not to worry. I go up to Sam and Roland and Marcus and Jimmy, and I thank them all and apologize for not being able to come through. They're all nice about it, but I feel like I've let them down as much as myself. Joe and I walk outside. I carry my guitar in its case.

"You let yourself beat you," Joe says.

I nod.

"I think the first song came out right because I kept it simple. I tried to top myself on the other two."

Joe points to my head.

"You were singing from there when you should have been singing from your heart."

We stand on the sidewalk. The light turns green, and another wave of cars rolls past. People are getting off work and going home.

He puts a hand on my shoulder and says, "We'll go back into the studio this week or next. You'll do fine. Don't you worry about it. I'll let you know when we can get everyone together."

We say goodbye, I put my guitar on the backseat and get in my car and drive. I don't remember where. I just drive and try not to think about it.

30

I GET HOME after eleven. Aunt Norma's in the kitchen. A cigarette burns between her fingers. I set my guitar case on the floor.

"What are you doing up?"

"Couldn't sleep."

"What's the matter?"

"You got two calls around nine or so. It was that Harold Washington. I don't like you doing business with him."

"Harold? What did he say?"

"He said he found out something about that what's his name, Albert Cuffee. He said it was important and to go to his office as soon as you get in."

"He said that?"

"Yes, but wait till morning."

"If Harold called it's serious."

She balls her fists into the elbows of her robe and says, "It's past eleven o'clock."

"He'd only call if it's urgent."

I leave the house and get back in my car. Albert Cuffee was a name I didn't expect to hear. But Harold had gone to the trouble so I couldn't just let it go. I pull up and see a police car in front of the liquor store below Harold's office. I park and get out. A crowd stands on the sidewalk. A cop I know is guarding the door.

"Marty, what's going on?"

"Big mess. Neeley's up there now."

The blood drains from my face.

"Was it Harold?"

"Yeah, you know him?"

"We've worked together. Let me in."

Marty checks if anyone's watching, then nods me through. I run up the stairs. The door's open. The cop jumps as I enter and says, "What are you doing here?"

"Are you Neeley?"

"You a reporter?"

"No. Harold's my friend"

"Friend?"

"We worked together."

"Who the hell are you?"

I show him my license.

"Just don't touch anything."

It's a bloodbath. Lotte's tied face down over Harold's desk. Her legs are spread apart and her dress cut open. A piece is stuffed in her mouth. Harold's tied to his chair. His eyes bulge from his head. Their throats are cut ear to ear. Their blood puddles on the floor. The cop opens the window; the sound of the street rushes in with the air.

"Niggers," he says. "Look how they do each other."

I turn around. He points to a small set of scales. It's twisted and stepped on.

"Harold's been dealing heroin on someone else's turf," he says.

"Heroin? Harold? He may have sold reefer, but never to whites."

"Well there's two bindles under the desk. Mexican black tar."

The cop points his thumb at Harold and Lotte.

"And whoever did this made sure nobody would ever try to move in on their territory again."

I shake my head and say, "Harold left a message for

me two hours ago about a case I was working on. He told me to come. He's no dope peddler."

Detective Parnham enters the room.

"What case? Someone's stolen Chevy? This doesn't concern you, Rhodeen."

I've never hit a cop but I came close. Then Marty calls out, "Hey Detective, this kid saw something."

We turn to the door. Standing next to Marty is a small colored boy. He trembles. His daddy holds his hand and says, "Tell 'em what you seen."

The boy begins to mumble.

"Speak up now, son. These men aren't gonna hurt you."

"I was running an errand. Two men rushed out the door. They jumped in a car."

Parnham crouches down by the boy. He places a hand on the boy's shoulder.

"Did you get a look at them?"

"Just one."

"What did he look like?"

"He was big. His hand was bleeding. He looked like a bear."

"A bear?"

"Yeah. Big body, big head, little eyes. Like a bear."

"What about the car?"

The boy closes his eyes.

"It was white. No, blue."

"Was one of them the driver?"

"No, it was someone else."

Parnham rubs the kid's head.

"Thank you, boy."

"Marty, get their names. Tomorrow, I want him to look at some mug shots."

Neeley clears his throat and says, "There's still the

heroin."

I shake my head and leave. I walk downstairs and into the crowd. They stand on their toes, hoping to see blood. They make it hard for me to pass. I see Harold's sister, Bella, running in the street. She's thickset and wears a coral-colored dress. She runs without any shoes. I double back and tell Marty not to let her inside. I push my way through the mob. Bella's eyes are inflamed.

"Bella, it's me. Tommy."

"Tommy, it true?"

"They were murdered. The cops say they were dealing heroin, but that ain't right."

"Heroin? That's bullsheeit."

"I know. Something's going on. Harold left me a message earlier. About a case I was working on. I came and found this."

"He left you a message about one of your recovery deals?"

I lower my head.

"And Harold got killed? You get the hell out of here."

31

MOURNERS FILL the sidewalk in front of the CME church on Linden Avenue. They stare at me as I pass through them. I hear murmuring and cursing. I hear ugly words I know are not true. Someone grabs my elbow. I wheel around expecting to get hit. It's Bella's husband, Larry.

"Tommy, you can't go in there. Bella blames you. So do a lot of other folks. Harold liked you. And you him. But you're not family."

Larry's right. I tell him I'm sorry for his loss. I say some other things. But there's nothing for me to do but go home. I remember my momma's funeral as I drive. I was seven. People thought they could say things to change the way I felt. They said things like I just told Larry, things that only made me feel worse. At my momma's service, I pretended to be someplace else.

I go home. I see a message from Evelyn in the kitchen. But I don't want to speak with anyone, even her. In my room I stare where two cracks meet in the ceiling. A mosquito hawk presses itself flat against the wall. The sunlight on the shade grows dim.

*   *   *

There's a knock on my door. It opens. Evelyn stands in the doorway.

"Tommy, I heard what happened. About Harold."

I turn to face the wall and close my eyes. I feel the bed sag. She places her hand on my head.

"I'm sorry. I know you're angry and you feel responsible for what happened to Harold. And that you'd do anything to bring him back. I know what it's like to lose someone. But I want you to come back to me."

I keep my eyes closed. I don't speak. I can't speak. I feel the bed rise as Evelyn gets up and I hear her feet cross the floor. I open my eyes and look at the wall. I think about what she said and realize she's right. Not just about Harold. I was jealous of Elvis. I could never be him. And I wasn't even all that good as a private investigator. But Evelyn still—

"You're going to mope around all day when you got a pretty girl who loves you?"

I turn over and see Aunt Norma standing in the doorway, her arms crossed.

"I've never known a boy who enjoys grief as much as you. You remember when your daddy sent that yardman away? You moped around for two weeks saying how much he meant to you. Then you never mentioned him again. And now you cry more for these two niggers than when your own momma died."

I jump out of bed.

"I was seven years old! You think I didn't care?"

Aunt Norma sets her hands on her hips.

"You took those little toy trucks out of your pocket and you played with them on the ground at your momma's burial. And you only cried when your daddy took them away."

"She was my momma. You think I wasn't sad? Look at you. What makes you an expert?"

Aunt Norma puts her hand to her throat. I keep talking, the words pour out.

"You never had any kids of your own. You just moved in after momma died and you—"

"You little beast. I took care of you and your daddy. I put the two of you ahead of me. Oh, you're a mean one."

Tears run down her face. I feel awful and ashamed. I step forward and touch her arm. "I'm sorry," I say. "Please forgive me."

Aunt Norma wipes her eyes. She nods her head, opens her arms, and hugs me.

32

PARNHAM CALLS the next morning. He tells me to come downtown. I stop to get cigarettes. On the shelf behind the cashier are brown paper bags of nuts; I buy some pistachios. I continue on to Central and park my car in the lot across from the courthouse.

Detective Parnham sits at his desk. He closes the file he's reading, tells me to sit down, and thanks me for coming.

As I sit in the chair, I toss the bag of pistachios onto his desk. It slides several inches and stops; anymore and it will drop in Parnham's lap. He shakes his head and smiles as he reaches for the bag. He tears it open, pulls out a handful, and smirks. Then he pushes the bag to me and says, "All right, tell me about Harold and Lotte."

I get some pistachios and say, "They never sold heroin."

"Then why were they murdered? Why the two bindles and that set of scales?"

"Did they have their fingerprints?"

"No, but that don't prove—"

"Don't prove what?"

"You said Harold left you a message?"

I look at the floor and mumble.

"What? Speak up."

"About an old case," I say.

"What was it?"

"That's confidential."

He shakes his head.

"Your friends are dead and you don't want to talk about it."

I stare at Parnham. He cracks a pistachio and says, "I'll split you open like one of these nuts." He tosses the shell into the ashtray and continues speaking:

"You used to hang out with Bob Oakley and Jim Gantry, right? I hear Bob got out of prison. How many years he do? Oh, never mind, that's old news."

Parnham smiles.

"Jim though… He's new news. Sold amphetamines to some truck driver. That son-of-a-bitch trucker caused a pileup. He'll live. The other people aren't so lucky. Jim's downstairs. You can keep him company."

I feel like I'm about to throw up.

"It's Jim's second time to the dance so he's being real friendly. He told us where he was getting the stuff. He even gave us the names of some of his favorite customers. He mentioned you."

My heart goes out to the folks this trucker killed, but I can't believe Jim would give me up.

"You gonna believe a drug dealer?" I say.

"You want to appear in court? Fine by me. I'll get that guy to testify you've been receiving and selling stolen merchandise. You'll not just lose that P.I. license, you'll go to prison."

I stop trying to open a pistachio. I set it down and say, "I'd been looking for a girl. Her parents hired me to."

"Now, how hard was that?"

I look back at the floor.

"Where did you find her?"

"I didn't."

"You didn't?"

"She sent her parents a letter. They let it go at that."

"You think I'm fooling, Rhodeen?"

He picks up the phone and says, "Let's see if Jim wants company."

"I'm telling the truth. You've never had a case end funny?"

"Okay, Rhodeen. But if you lied I'll chew you up and spit you out. So what do you think Harold wanted to tell you?"

"I wish I knew."

Parnham gets another handful of pistachios. He slides the bag to me and says, "You guys were friends."

I nod.

"You didn't know Sigmund, did you?"

"He was your partner," I say.

"That's right. He walked into a liquor store. He was off duty. There was a holdup. It ended badly. None of the witnesses would testify. I took care of it."

I stare at Parnham, my mouth hangs open. He opens a folder and takes out the photos of Harold and Lotte, the ones taken that night. Parnham sets them down so I can see them and says, "That colored boy looked through the mug shots."

I stare at the photos and the detective keeps talking:

"He ID'd the guy."

My palms get sweaty. I look up at the detective.

"Charlie Griggs. Enforcer and loan collector, mostly. They all pay when he shows up."

Parnham slides the folder to me. I open it. I take out the mugshots and stare into the face of a killer. He's a big man with a big head and small eyes, and I can see why the kid says he looks like a bear.

"Charlie got out of Brushy Mountain last October," Parnham says. "He kept a room at the Marquette. We turned it over. He left town."

"How do you know?"

"He's from Houston. It says in that file he always goes back when there's trouble. Already sent a teletype, but I don't expect it will do much good. He's got a bunch of cousins that'll keep him hid."

Parnham leans back in his chair. He stretches his arms and says, "Years ago, I'd heard about Griggs's daddy. That Jesse did crazy stuff, like ride up to Shreveport or Deep Ellum and knock over whorehouses. Till he picked the wrong one. This madam, Minnie Shelton, took shit from no one. Minnie popped Jesse in the belly with a derringer. Point blank range. She laid the gun on the bar and picked up a spoon. She sat on his chest and scooped out his eyes. Then she fed Jesse to the hogs. Minnie never got charged. No evidence."

It was a horrible story, but what happened to Griggs's daddy didn't excuse what he did to Harold and Lotte. Besides, Harold told me plenty of stories about growing up on his stepdaddy's farm. That was barbaric, but Harold had put that behind him. He didn't need some vicious hired killer for him to know pain.

"Yeah, I expect Charlie's already in Houston by now," Parnham says. "And what's more… turns out that colored kid and his family are gone. Moved out. Can't blame them. Not many people would testify against Griggs."

"There's a duplicate set of photos," I say. "Can I take one?"

"Be my guest."

33

I GET PACKED. I grab Dale's pistol. But I need money. I leave a note for Aunt Norma, telling her I'll be gone for a while. I have only one stop before I leave town.

Sid Bernstein stands behind his counter polishing a silver bowl. He has on a rumpled shirt. A cigarette sits in the corner of his mouth; the ash has smeared across his vest. He looks up as I walk into his shop.

"Tommy, good to see you."

"You, too, Sid."

"Rabbi Waxman told me you got the pointer back."

I nod my head.

He looks down at the guitar case in my hand.

"You need something?"

I open the case. Sid parks his cigarette in the tray. He picks up the Gretsch. He inspects the guitar and drags a fingernail over the strings.

"It's a beauty. You're going to reclaim it, right?"

"Right now I need the money."

"I can give you a hundred and seventy-five dollars."

I reach into my pocket and take out the silk bag. Sid screws a jeweler's loupe into his eye and examines the cufflinks.

"They'll bring it up to three hundred."

I nod and point to the rest.

"The wedding bands? I have so many just like them. The best I can do is forty-five. They were your parents'?"

"Write the ticket," I say.

Sid does the paperwork. He hands me the money and a pawn ticket. I look at the guns on the shelf.

"Do you have any extra magazines for a .45? And a box of ammo?"

He raises his eyebrows and says, "Are you in some kind of trouble?"

"Are you gonna sell them to me or not?"

"I just don't want you to get hurt."

I set my hands on the counter and look into his eyes. Sid crushes his cigarette in the tray. He looks at me and picks some flakes of tobacco off his tongue. As he walks into the back he says, "I don't normally sell ammunition."

Sid comes back, lays a magazine and a box of Winchesters on the counter. I get out my wallet.

"I don't want your money for that."

I thank Sid and leave. I get in my car and head south.

As I blow past the Mississippi state line, I swallow two of Jim's pills. I have five more left. I drive alongside cotton fields. I see chickens peck for bugs in front of a shack. I speed past barbecue joints and roadhouses and roadkill broiling on the tarmac. Grasshoppers splat across the windshield, green and gray. Armed guards on horseback watch over a chain gang clearing brush along the road.

Up ahead I see a sign for gas at a four-corners and I pull in. The sun and wind have long stripped the paint off the building. Sweat rolls down my back as I step out of the car. I peel down to my undershirt. The boy comes out from under the shade. He pumps the gas up into the cylinder to fill my tank. He cleans the windshield as I go in to pay. A ceiling fan churns the heavy air, making a fly strip rotate. Two old fellas nod at me as I get a grape Nehi out of the icebox. I pay the cashier who says, "You come back now," as I leave. I finish the drink and return the bottle before I get back on the road.

Barefoot colored kids wave at me from beside the highway, and I wonder if they'd ever been more than ten miles from where they stand.

At Mound Bayou, I get off the highway and head away from town. Small dark figures bend over on the horizon. They haul long sacks they'll repeatedly fill with cotton. The endless work seems absurd, but hunger causes people to do anything. I turn onto a dirt road, drive another mile, and roll by a scuppernong vine ripening on a fence. I pull over and kill the engine.

I get out of the car. The raw sunlight scorches the land. I open the trunk and take out the gun and walk into the field. The wind kicks up from the rows of cotton, pelting me with grit. I walk. I walk under the white sun.

The top of an old bottle pokes through the soil. I toe it out with my shoe, pick it up, and set it on the bank of a gully where the water pools before it flows into a culvert. I pace off five yards and chamber a round. I aim at the bottle. The blast jerks my arm. The bottle sits untouched. I step forward and fire. Dirt explodes two feet away from it. I halve the distance, fire twice and miss. Sweat and tears roll down my face. I can't hit the bottle. I throw it in the water.

I sit on the ground with my hands on my face. I was in the army, but never in battle. In the Bible it says the fining pot is for silver and the furnace for gold, but the Lord trieth the hearts. But men too are tested by fire and until I am, I'm no match for Charlie Griggs.

I drive back. I drive back into Tennessee. I go clear cross Memphis and keep going. A string of cars and trucks are parked along the roadside. I slow down. I hear singing coming up from the Loosahatchie. I pull over to see what it's about. I follow the footpath down to the river and come upon a group of people singing a hymn. Several stand soaking wet with the clothes on their back dripping in the sun. I look beyond. Two men stand in the river on either side of a lady. The taller man speaks:

"This is something Shirley here tells us is missing in her life. Praise the Lord! And so she wants to be baptized. Amen! And to feel the righteousness flow from the top of her head all the way down to the tips of her toes. Whoa! And so Shirley we now baptize you in the name of the father and the son and the Holy Ghost!"

And as he finishes his oration, the two men tilt the lady back. Her head goes under the water. Her blonde hair floats fan-like upon the surface. They raise her up. With water streaming from her hair and face, she smiles and uses her thumb and forefinger to clear her nose. The people begin to sing and two enter the river to help her out. An old man in a pair of khakis nods to me. The lines in his face show he works under the sun.

"You been baptized?" he asks.

"I don't know. I was too young to remember."

"You don't remember? Then it was ain't done right."

I smile and shake my head. He steps to me and places a hand on my shoulder.

"When your house is on fire you gonna drip some well-water on it and call it done? Well, the house of your soul is on Hellfire, son. And less you get right with Jesus, you're gonna burn when the time comes."

Another one's plunged into the river and I point there.

"You been baptized? Like that?"

"Sure have."

"And that makes everything all right?"

"In the hereafter."

"What about now?"

The old man shakes his head and mutters. I look

toward the riverbank. Identical twin boys, about sixteen years old, get ready to receive their ablutions.

He points his finger at me and says, "When you bury the dead, you just gonna toss a little dirt on 'em? Or you gonna bury 'em deep?"

I don't reply. He walks away.

Someone chuckles behind me. I turn around. It's a man, he's in his forties. A narrow brim straw fedora sits on his head. He holds a jacket over his shoulder.

"You been baptized?" I ask.

"Yeah, but in church not in that river."

"Then why are you here?"

He mops his forehead with a handkerchief and smiles.

The baptism ends and the people leave. The natural sounds of the river return. I sit by the water. I hear a splash and turn to see a set of circles ripple across the surface. A dark shape materializes below and disappears. On the opposite shore, a great blue heron cocks its head. The bird lunges into the shallows and brings up a frog. It wriggles in the heron's beak. I brush the sand from my pants and climb up the path. My car's the only one left.

I drive north. The road's familiar and I realize I'm not far from the Williams's cabin. I get on the dirt road and, by force of habit, chose the right fork. I cut the engine. It's that time between late afternoon and early evening. I sit in the car, watching a pair of squirrels chase each other up and around a tree. I'm about to restart the car, but I came this far. I get out and walk up the dirt road to the cabin. No cars sit out front.

I no longer have the key. I hadn't thought about how to get in. I walk around the place and notice one of the windows is ajar. I peer inside. The room looks empty. I lift the window and pull myself in.

On the couch, I sit in the dark and smoke a cigarette. I

study the orange glow as I think about how I need to change. I need to get over my fear to go up against Charlie Griggs.

I don't hear the car pull up, just the engine dying and the doors slam. A girl giggles. I'm finally going to meet Helen Williams. I put out my cigarette and wait. The keys jingle. The bolt turns. The door opens and a couple stands briefly in silhouette. A pair of boots struts in the dark. A match sparks and the lantern lights the room. Dale Martins stands beneath it. And where I expect to see Helen is her cousin, June.

I get up from the couch and say, "Hello."

Dale jumps.

"Why are you here?"

"Why are you?" I reply.

I walk toward them.

"Why didn't you invite Dale to your recital?" I ask.

June makes a face like I've pissed in the punchbowl and says, "That's a stupid thing to say."

"I guess that makes me a stupid guy."

She gives a snort, and Dale turns to her and says, "Don't you go making things worse."

June smiles and takes a step toward me. She places her hand on my cheek.

"Now, you're not going to tell Aunt Claire and Uncle Garland about us, are you?"

"No, why should I spoil it?"

It isn't the answer they're expecting. They don't say anything. I leave before I change my mind. I go home.

34

MY HORSE LIKES to eat grass. I've ridden Slick all season long and I've not been able to break him of this habit. He's a three-year-old gelding; a bay dun Morgan with a black mane, forelock, and tail. His forelimbs are also dark and banded. He's a handsome horse and, despite his taste for grass and bad habits, I'm lucky to ride him.

I pull up on the reins to get his face out of the grass, and he bolts as if he's been spooked, spurred, and struck by lightning all at the same time. I hold on. He gallops through the tall grass. I'm like a crop duster flying above a field.

Slick finally slows down. He slows because he can't breathe. I step off the horse and see that Slick's nose has swollen shut. He can't get air through his nostrils. They have fang marks that are about a half an inch apart. Slick has been bit by a rattlesnake in the grass.

I was riding by myself. The ranch is about twelve miles away. I've never doctored a snake-bit horse. I don't know what to do. Slick's eyes roll back into his head. Slobber pours from his mouth, and his muscles begin to twitch. Slick is my horse; I'd been made responsible for him. I let him get away with his bad habits, and now he's in trouble. I'm in trouble.

Slick begins to buckle and he lies in the grass. His lips have disappeared. I cut the halter and bridle off his head and pull out the bit, but horses can't breathe through their mouths. His wheezing gets heavier and he begins to convulse.

Helplessly, I gawk into Slick's eyes. They roll down for a moment and then flip back up into his skull. What they see there, I don't know. His nose continues to swell, blocking any air from getting into his lungs.

His convulsions slow down. Slick shudders and goes silent. I sit with my back against his and cry. I'm only a boy. I'm fourteen. I've heard there's a way to cut open a horse's nose if it's bitten, but I don't know how. And I was too scared to try. I failed.

The sun will soon drop behind the mountains. I have to get moving. I work my saddle off him and take the carbine out of the scabbard. I take a last look at Slick. I no longer cry.

I pull the saddle up over my shoulder and hold it by the horn. I carry the carbine in my left hand. I leave the blanket, my canteen, and some other things behind. I head down the grade toward the creek; I'll follow it to get to the ranch. Later, I'll need to cross the river. I'll figure that out when I got there.

It's hard. Walking is hard. Walking is something you don't do when you work on a ranch, unless it's to get in line for chow. What's more, I'm carrying a saddle that weighs nearly thirty pounds and a carbine that weighs close to seven. I have to stop and rest many times. When I get to the creek, I lie on my belly and drink. After I have my fill, I walk beside the water.

I should have returned hours ago. The work I haven't done will be noticed, and I halfway hope that Mark or one of the other hands will come and find me along the way. It's bad enough I'm coming back without my horse; I can't come back without my saddle.

Slick and I had ridden past here earlier in the day, and

we had come across the remains of an elk near where a brook runs into the creek. But I wasn't thinking about that now. I'm thinking about what my father will say when I get back without my horse. How his face will look at mine, the disappointment visible in his gray eyes. Slick may have been mine because I rode him, but Slick belonged to my father. He had bought him and four other horses at an auction outside Cody. Horses are not cheap; they are not toys.

I look up. The sun stands above the mountaintops, and from where the snow had melted only some months ago. The shadows will be coming soon. The breeze picks up and I smell what's left of the elk. A raven flies up into a pine and squawks. My shoulder feels sore and my hands hurt. I stop and set down the saddle.

The sound gets its attention. I hear a bone snap and I see the grizzly rise from the other side of the downed elk. Its mouth, claws, and chest are black with blood. Saliva hangs from its jaws. It stares at me with its small eyes. They look blank, like two pieces of black plastic sewn into a toy. I see nothing in its eyes. Then the grizzly rushes over the top of the elk and charges me. I lever the carbine and fire into the bear's chest. The bear keeps coming. I lever another round and pull the trigger as the grizzly comes crashing down on me.

I sit up in bed. I had heard a gun. I think it was a dream. I'm not sure. I fall back to sleep.

*   *   *

I go to Sid's in the morning to redeem my pawn ticket. I come home and put my guitar under my bed. I need to become a man who'd go up against Charlie Griggs. I need to be that man. But something else crosses my mind. Was

Dale being straight with me about Helen? Mrs. Williams seemed convinced it was him. And seeing Dale with June, I just didn't know.

That night I go to find out. It had rained most of the day, but it stops as I get in line at the theater. I ask the girl in the ticket booth for Dale. She tells me he called in sick. I get back in my car. I drive to the building where I'd seen him before, that first night I followed him home.

I park in front of the radio repair shop; it takes up the ground floor of the building. In the window is a TV set, and a wrestling match flickers on the screen. The door to the stairs is unlocked. I go in. I look at the mailboxes to find the number for Dale's apartment. The place smells dank from the mold and of greasy cooking odors. I climb the stairs and walk down the hall. I knock. The door opens. Dale stands in an undershirt. His hair lays plastered on his head.

"What the hell do you want?"

"A word."

He lets me in, and as he closes the door he shrugs and says, "I thought you were the delivery boy. The chicken place around the corner."

Dale sits on the edge of a sofa; the fabric is worn and faded. I step over a stack of dirty plates, move some magazines off a chair and sit down.

"So why are you here?" Dale asks.

"Did you tell me the truth? About you and Helen?"

Dale looks at me and sighs. I watch his eyes as he answers.

"You ever hear of a guy bragging he didn't score?"

I shake my head. I made a mistake. He was telling me the truth. He always had. I'd only been distracting myself from what I really needed to do. I shouldn't have come.

"So you're sick?" I ask as something more to say.

"Yeah, I woke up with a fever. Hey, what about my gun? I want it back."

I smile and say, "Next time."

There's a knock at the door. Dale gets up and says, "My supper. You hungry?" as he undoes the latch.

I hear three pops. Dale groans and falls against the door, pushing it shut. I leap up and turn him over. Blood covers his bathrobe. He looks like a bag of dirty laundry. Dale has a hole in his forehead, two more in the belly.

I yank open the door, run down the stairs, and onto the street. The rain's falling. An arm thrusts over the roof of a car. Two flashes hurl out of the darkness. The air rips over my head.

The gunman's shoes clack on the sidewalk. I follow. He rounds the corner. I charge after him. I peer from behind the wall. He's vanished into the rain. I run in a crouch, up against the parked cars, watching and listening for where he's gone. Up ahead, a car door opens. A man and a lady step out. They argue under their umbrella. I yell at them to get back in their car. I yell again. They can't hear from the rain. I race past them as a shape slides from behind a mailbox. Two more bullets speed my way. The lady screams. She and the man dive between two parked cars.

The gunman runs and I dash after. He pivots around. I see a flash. Broken bits of asphalt hit me in the shins. He runs straight at me, laughing, his arm outstretched. A truck tosses him into the air, then skids to a stop. The man falls. His limbs stick out in the wrong direction. I crouch down. His face looks familiar. I touch his hair. Dye rubs off on my hand. I sniff.

"Shoe polish," I say. It's the bellhop. The one I had seen with Mrs. Williams.

A police car pulls up and two officers jump out. The

truck driver covers his face with his hands and says it was an accident. I show my P.I. license to the cops. I tell them to radio Parnham. I have a story to tell.

35

THE ROOM IS COLD, and the pale green walls fade into shadows like the colors of a three-day-old bruise. I sit across from Parnham while his boss, Lieutenant Fessenden, batters me with questions. A black metal desk lamp creates a harsh pool of light on the grubby wooden table in front of me. On the table are cups of coffee, an ashtray, and a pile of evidence taken from the bellhop. There's his wallet, a scrap of paper with Dale's address, a .32 caliber pistol, and a pass key from the Claridge hotel.

I retell the story for a third time. I tell them about Helen's disappearance, and being hired to find her, and how she used to go with Dale. I tell them about the honey-colored woman and how I got Helen's letter, and how Mrs. Williams thought it was Dale who got Helen pregnant. I tell them why I think she's wrong.

I tell them how I saw Mrs. Williams and the bellhop at the Claridge, and about our conversation afterward. I tell them everything except about going after Charlie Griggs.

I tell them how Dale and June surprised me in the cabin. And why I went to see Dale this evening. But Fessenden isn't buying it.

"You expect me to charge the wife of a leading businessman with solicitation of murder without a single bit of evidence?"

I try to explain, but Fessenden puts out his hand.

"Hell, no, kid. We turned over that dump Dale lived in. We didn't find any hijacked Hollywood movies. We found 8mm films, the kind they show at stag parties."

I look at Parnham. He avoids my eyes and picks at his fingers. Fessenden keeps talking:

"And the kid who did in Dale. The bellhop. Donnie Simms. Let's say Donnie was setting up stag parties where he worked. Let's say that those two clowns had an argument. Then one up and dies of lead poisoning. And the other caught a truck for his final taxi."

I reach for my cigarettes and realize I'm out.

"Let's say that's what happened," Fessenden says. "Not some tall tale about a gal hiring her gigolo to murder the man she thinks knocked up her daughter. So dammit, I'm not going to investigate into respectable people like the Williamses. You understand?"

I point at the scrap of paper with Dale's address.

"If the two worked together and were partners, like you say, then why would the bellhop need that?"

Fessenden leans back. He turns toward Parnham. Parnham stops picking his fingers and says, "I'm going to get cigarettes."

The detective gets up and walks out the door. Fessenden removes the cellophane from a cigar and lights it. He taps the table a few times. Then he picks up the paper with Dale's address. He strikes a match and holds the flame under the paper. Wisps of smoke rise, it begins to smolder. The handwriting disappears as the paper turns into ash. He drops it into the tray. Fessenden stares me in the eye and says, "Why would the bellhop need what?"

I understand. I look at Fessenden. His face is placid.

The door opens and Parnham tiptoes in and sets a cup of coffee in front of his boss. He offers me a cigarette.

"They do that at firing squads," I say.

"We won't need that," Fessenden replies as he lights a match. He extends the flame toward me.

I take a puff.

Fessenden tosses the match and says, "I'll need you to sign a statement."

"Whatever you want."

"Come back in the morning," he says. "It can wait."

*   *   *

I wake early. I go back downtown to sign the statement. On the way out, a reporter stops me on the staircase. He asks me for a quote about the killings. Seems he'd read the statement before I had. I elbow past him, but he calls after me as I hustle to the parking lot. I get in my car and start it. Someone knocks. It's Parnham. He's waving, so I kill the engine. He opens the door, slides in and says, "Last night, I'm sorry about that."

I leave my hands on the wheel; I don't say anything. Parnham pats my knee and says, "Take me for a ride. I need to tell you something."

I turn the key. We roll out of the lot. He waits till we're in traffic before he speaks:

"I heard back from Houston P.D."

"About Griggs?"

"About his cousin, Marvin."

"Marvin?"

"He ran a heroin ring. Mexican black tar. You were right, Harold wasn't selling dope. Griggs just made it look that way. Anyhow they busted Marvin, two of his brothers, and some of his cousins last week. With Marvin busy, we think Charlie's gone someplace else. St. Louis or Chicago."

"Why are you telling me this?"

"Thought you'd want to know."

"What about your boss?"

"He doesn't give a damn about Griggs. I thought you did."

"I don't want to sign any more statements."

"I thought you wanted to go after Griggs for what he did to Harold and Lotte. That's why I let you have his mug shots."

"I started to. I didn't get far. But I will. But who are you to judge? You walked away while your boss burned evidence."

"Fessenden? You don't want to go up against him."

"What are you saying?"

"I've said enough."

I come to a stoplight. Parnham gets out. The light turns green. The guy behind me leans on his horn.

36

I WENT TO A COLORED PLACE that night on Beale Street. An old man plays a dobro. He sings and beats his foot on the floor to keep time. Someone taps me on the shoulder. I turn. It's Bella's husband, Larry.

"Can I sit with you?"

"Please do," I say.

He sits down across from me. We each take a swig of our beer.

"Sorry you had to miss Harold and Lotte's funeral."

"Well, me being there wasn't right."

Larry nods and takes a cigarette from his pack. He pats himself for matches. I pass him my cigarette; he uses it to get a light.

"You're famous," Larry says. "I read about you in the paper. You witness some dude shoot his partner dead. And the shooter gets hit by a truck."

I puff my cigarette and shake my head.

"One hundred percent pure bullshit."

Larry laughs and says, "I'll say. Who the fuck brings a gun to a truck fight?"

Then he gets serious and says, "I think I know what Harold wanted to tell you. What got him killed."

I set down my beer. Larry looks over his shoulder. He turns back to me and says, "This Albert Cuffee, worked for Garland Williams."

"He was his driver."

Larry nods. As he exhales he says, "He was also

Garland and Edward's face on a bunch of deals. Buying land on the cheap from colored folk. Deals no one would take if they knew who was behind 'em."

"You think someone who got ripped off got rid of Cuffee?"

"Yeah. In a manner of speaking. I hear Cuffee got greedy."

"You think it was the Williamses?"

"That's what it points to."

Larry glances over his shoulder.

"Now that leaves what happened to Harold and Lotte. Same people who done in Albert, done in them."

"We should talk to his wife," I say. "See what we can find."

Larry finishes his beer. He sets down the bottle and says, "Ain't no time like the present."

We get up and take my car. I remember the way. A few lights are on in the house. We walk through the gate. A dog barks across the street as I knock. Someone turns off a television and pretends not to be home. I knock again.

"Who is it?"

"Tommy Rhodeen."

"Who?"

"Tommy Rhodeen. Can we talk to you?"

Mrs. Cuffee unlocks the door. She looks out and says, "Who's that there with you?"

"A friend. Larry Baker."

"Why's he with you?"

"He's got an interest in your husband."

She lets us in. There are changes since I'd been there, including brand new furniture and a TV. Mrs. Cuffee tells her children to go to the bedroom.

"What do you want?"

"Albert was Garland Williams's driver," I say.

"That's right."

"But he did other work for the Williams brothers. It involved real estate. Did he speak with you about that?"

"I don't want no trouble. Mr. Williams been real good to me."

Larry turns on the TV; it's warm and the screen flickers awake as he says, "Lot of people not had it so good because of Albert and the Williamses."

"I don't know nothing about that."

I lean forward.

"People are gonna learn the truth. They're gonna find out who bought their land. They're gonna blame Albert, but they're gonna come see you."

"You think one of them did something to Albert?"

"We think Albert may have cheated the Williamses."

Mrs. Cuffee begins to cry. I change the subject.

"I don't see your momma. She okay?"

Mrs. Cuffee looks confused.

"She down the street. Why you ask about her for?"

"Nothing. I was just asking."

I get up and turn off the TV. I come back and set my hand on her arm and say, "The truth can be painful."

She gets on her feet as soon as the words are out of my mouth.

"You come into my home and try to make me feel small. I gots six kids to feed. You know what that's like? You accept what's offered. You don't ask so many questions. So unless you been on the other end of that deal, you should count yourself blessed."

There's nothing we could say. Two of her kids begin to cry in the next room. Mrs. Cuffee opens the front door and says, "I'd like you to leave now."

I slide under the steering wheel and start the engine. I

drop Larry off at his house, but I'm too keyed up to go home. I drive to Evelyn's. I want to tell her I'm sorry, and to just see her, but it's after midnight and the house is dark. I park in front, hoping I'll see Evelyn turn on a light. After half an hour, I get back on the road.

As I drive, I think about what Mrs. Cuffee told us. And, as much as I hoped she'd tell us what she knew, I can't fault her for keeping quiet. I roll to a stop at an intersection and realize I missed my turn. The light turns green. The guy in front doesn't move. The car behind me presses against my bumper. I'm trapped.

I jump out. Three colored men hop out of the cars and surround me. One comes forward. I give him two quick jabs and a right cross to the nose. Then another pulls a sack over my head from behind. I stomp my heel on his toe. The man curses and the pressure lets off. But I can't get the sack off me. And I don't see the punches that come next. I hit the ground. All goes black.

37

"YOU BEEN PUTTIN' your nose where it don't belong, Bright Eyes. You don't like your nose?"

I know the voice. It's the honey-colored woman who gave me Helen's letter. I open my eyes. She leans over me and says, "How'd you sleep?"

"I've slept better."

"I bet you have."

I try to move. My wrists and ankles are tied to a cot. I'm in a basement. Rhythm and blues comes through the ceiling, the sound muffled. My face feels puffy, my body bruised. She gets up and pours herself a drink. I see some guys sitting on crates against the wall. Despite the dim light, I recognize them as the men from the shack. One holds a bloody rag to his nose.

"I thought we made it clear to you. Stop puttin' your nose into people's bidness."

"Is that what Harold and Lotte did? Or what about Albert Cuffee?"

"Well, they lost more than their nose."

She turns around and picks something off the table. It's a syringe. She grips my arm. I shake it loose, but the cords prevent me from pushing her away.

"Hold him!" she yells at the men.

They get off their crates. I thrash harder as they near me. Two of the men place their hands on my shoulders and arms. The other one grabs my shins and he leans all his weight into me; a leer spreads across his face. I can't move. She bends down over me.

"Ever shot up before, Bright Eyes?"

She smiles and wraps a belt around my arm.

"You gonna like this."

She injects the heroin into my vein. I feel a warmness fill my body as my eyes close.

*　　　*　　　*

I'm wet. I try to open my eyes. They're stuck shut with mucous. I squeeze them tight, then relax. I do it again. Light begins to show through. I see better with my right. The honey-colored woman stands above me holding a pail. She sets it down and wipes my face with a rag.

"How you feelin' Bright Eyes?"

"Not so good."

"Yeah, you doing okay. Last time, I didn't need anyone t'hold you down. I think you like the stuff."

She holds up a mirror. My wasted face looks back.

"You look like a dope fiend," she says. "And when we dump what's left of you on the street, the only thing people gonna say is *junkie*."

She sticks me with her needle. It's as if I want her to. I feel the wave surge; it hits me and my eyes go heavy and shut.

"Hey, save some for me," I think I hear someone say.

"You a grown man, Charlie Griggs. Don't you think you got enough bad habits?"

The man shouts and there's a slap. I try to hold on, to listen, to hear the name again.

"What the hell you thinkin' woman! Using my name in front of him?"

I didn't hear anything more.

38

I LOSE TRACK of the days. How many times has she shot the heroin into my vein? I'm barely conscious when I'm awake. A single light bulb hangs from the ceiling. The edges of the room disappear into shadow. My arm's sore from the needle. My head burns with fever, and I lay in my own urine. They've untied and retied my arms and legs several times. I'm still tied to the cot, but now there's more play in the ropes. I need to escape. I thrust my left side against the cords. I use my arms and legs to rock myself over. On the fifth try, I'm on my belly with the cot on top of me. I feel my guts heave; I vomit face down on the concrete. I shiver and spit.

From the floor, I peer up at the top half of a bottle on a table. I crawl through my puke, the cot tied to my limbs. I grip the leg and shake the table. The bottle topples. It rolls. I close my eyes and hear it smash on the floor. Broken glass and whiskey spray over me. I look and see a long shard of glass attached to the bottle's neck. I stretch my arm toward it, then inch forward the rest of the way. I grasp its neck, slip the edge between the rope and my wrist and cut myself free. I expect to hear the door open and men race down the stairs. So far no one comes. I cut the other ropes off. And still no one comes into the basement.

I lean against the wall to wipe the vomit from my clothes. I discover my pockets are turned inside out. On the table I see my wallet. I pick it up; the cash is gone, but they left my identification. I stuff it into my pocket and move on. I know the stairs are ahead. I wobble forward and find the railing. I hang on to it as I climb up the stairwell in the dark. I feel for the knob, grasp it, and turn. The door's locked from the other side. I turn around and climb my way to the bottom to look for another way out.

Daylight seeps from the dirty window above my head. It's too small and too high to reach, and covered with bars. I grope for another exit. I step past wooden crates and cardboard boxes. Some are empty. Some hold liquor or beer. Everywhere, rodent droppings are scattered on the floor. In a corner lies the dented brass horn of a gramophone. It's next to a grandfather clock resting on its side. Its weights and pendulum are gone, and both its hands are missing.

I turn a corner. A man appears to sleep in a chair, his back is toward me. I lift a bottle out of a case of liquor and raise it over my head. I take another step and spot the syringe sticking out of the man's arm. It's Charlie Griggs. I push his shoulder. The syringe falls out, he crumples to the floor, his mouth hangs open. I look down at Griggs. There's things I would have told him, things I would have done, but it's too late. And I need to get moving.

On the wall is a switch. I push the button. It makes a whirring sound. The noise stops. Two doors open. It's a dumbwaiter; it smells of sour milk and rancid meat. I squeeze myself in, reach out, and push the button. The doors close, casting me into blackness. I wait for something to happen. A thud makes my guts heave as I rise, and I fight to keep my stomach down. The movement stops. The doors open. I lean out and vomit on the floor.

I lower myself out of the dumbwaiter. I'm in a kitchen. I'm alone. A clock on the wall shows it's just after five. Below the clock is a door. I slide the bolt and push it open. My eyes squint in the daylight, but the air from the alley feels good and it clears my head. I stagger to the street.

A taxicab slows down and the window lowers.

"You need a ride?"

I stumble into the cab and collapse on the seat.

"Where to?"

I hadn't thought of that. My only thought was to get out alive. I need a place to hide.

"Third Street. Between Exchange and Poplar."

The cabbie pulls off. He makes a U-turn in the empty street and drives on. I rub my eyes and ask, "What day is it?"

He looks at me in the mirror.

"How 'bout I take you to a hospital?"

"Hospital, no good."

"You need a doctor."

"Hospital, no good."

"Okay."

He prods me awake.

"Which is it buddy?"

I look.

"The apartment above the tailor's. I don't have any money."

The cabbie carries me across the street and rings the bell. I look worse than a bum, but I know I'll be okay. I hear footsteps. The door opens. Rabbi Waxman reaches out and holds me.

39

I OPEN my eyes. I lie in a bed with clean linen. Where? I don't know. I feel weak, but my mind begins to clear. The honey-colored woman. The heroin. Charlie Griggs. The taxi driver. The rabbi.

I touch my face. I've been cleaned and shaved. I feel alert. I think of Evelyn. I swivel my legs over the side of the bed. I stand up. My feet go out. I fall back. The door opens, and I see the rabbi.

"Tommy, you can't go anywhere like this."

I nod.

"Can you eat?"

I shake my head.

"But you must drink."

I nod again.

"I'll be right back."

Someone touches my shoulder. I open my eyes. The rabbi stands above me holding a glass of orange juice.

"Drink this. The sugar will help."

He holds the glass to my lips as I drink.

"Go back to sleep."

I do.

I wake up and for the third time find my head over a bucket. Each time I vomit I feel like I'm going to break. Then the rabbi makes me drink again. I get it down. I throw it up. I fall back to sleep.

*　　*　　*

I look up from the pillow. The rabbi sits in a chair.

"How are you feeling?"

"Better."

"Can you eat?"

"Yes."

He comes back with a bowl of soup and a piece of bread. I eat. I eat it all, but don't want more.

"Thank you," I say. "How long have I been here?"

"Three days now. What happened?"

"It started after that job I told you about. The one for a family on Morningside Place."

I tell him the entire story. The rabbi listens. He doesn't ask questions. I tell him everything, even about going after Charlie Griggs and that I was unable to do it. I tell him how I wound up in the basement and what happened to me, and how I escaped and found Griggs dead. The rabbi knows my story.

"So Albert helped the Williams brothers buy property at well-below value prices," the rabbi says. "They're politically connected people, are they not?"

"Very."

"So it's likely they had inside information."

"I read in the paper about highways. Something the government is doing."

The rabbi nods his head and says, "The Federal Aid Highway Act. The president signed the bill last month."

"They must've known about it long before then. They must've figured how to profit from it. They'll stop anyone who gets in their way."

"Is there anyone on the police force you trust?"

"Not after what's happened."

"What about Parnham?"

"He means well, but he won't go up against his boss."

The rabbi leans forward in his chair and puts his hand

to my forehead.

"We're not going to solve this tonight," he says, "but you're getting better."

"Yes, thank you."

"You need more sleep. I shouldn't keep you awake."

As he gets up I say, "There's something else that bothers me."

The rabbi waits for me to speak.

"I see how far people will go to get ahead. But when I look at myself, I realize I'm not all that innocent. I got my P.I. license because I helped a judge get back his dog. And I make money getting people back their stolen property."

The rabbi sits back in his chair and says, "Tommy, have people been harmed by you getting your license? Reuniting a judge with his dog and getting a piece of paper? You're comparing that with murder? A man and his dog? Tommy, what you did was a *mitzvah*. It means a praiseworthy act. So you got fast-tracked to getting your license. Were you not eligible to receive one?"

I shake my head.

"Then show me the harm? Life is not black and white. We deal with shades of gray. There are degrees. And you are being too hard on yourself."

I nod, perhaps he's right. The rabbi continues speaking:

"We're put on Earth to understand who we are and to do what is right. But life is to live."

I look at him and say, "You told me your granddaddy fought at Shiloh. What that was it like for him?"

"How does any man experience war? It was hell, but he was lucky. My granddaddy, Benjamin, was part of the surprise attack on Grant's army, but he got wounded the next day."

"I didn't know. Didn't you tell me he also fought at Chickamauga?"

He nods his head and says, "Chickamauga showed how the wrong information can change the course of history. General Rosecrans thought he had a gap in the line, so he ordered a division to fill it. But there was no gap. Until he created one by moving his men. Benjamin was where this gap appeared. General Longstreet ordered his troops forward. The assault forced Rosecrans to retreat."

The rabbi stands up. He walks as he speaks:

"Longstreet wanted to keep after Rosecrans, but it wasn't his decision. General Bragg was the commander. Nearly fifteen thousand of his men lay wounded after the battle, most unable to fight. Bragg decided to let Rosecrans get away. Instead, he laid siege to Chattanooga.

"But Grant overran Bragg, retaking the city just two months later. Consequently, Longstreet's unexpected victory at Chickamauga was all in vain.

"But maybe Bragg was right. Maybe he didn't have the men he needed to go after Rosecrans. It may have been the right decision."

I look at the rabbi and say, "I chickened out when I went after Charlie Griggs. And I said nothing when Fessenden burned evidence; I even signed his statement. But I won't let the Williamses get away with it."

The rabbi sits down. He looks up at the ceiling, then at me.

"You have in your mind a view of the world in which everything hinges on you. It's a belief that doesn't allow for options beyond your imagination and, more often than not, ends in sorrow. Many men see things this way and it's not an accurate view of the world. Do you understand what I'm saying?"

I nod my head.

"Benjamin was part of a regiment during those battles. He didn't charge the line single-handedly, which doesn't make what he did any less brave. But you're just one man. And there's a difference between bravery and foolhardy."

He gets up and sits next to me on the bed and says, "Great men are often seen at a distance. What I mean is that we view them through our own experiences and not through the lives in which they actually led. Despite his successes, Benjamin Waxman died an unhappy man because he did not achieve the one thing he truly cared about. I understand how you feel. We'll talk again in the morning."

I GET OUT of bed at a quarter to five. I find my clothes cleaned and hanging in the closet. I get dressed. I creep down the hall and spot the rabbi's car keys. There's a pad of paper; I leave a note.

I park his car around the block from my house. Aunt Norma hears me come inside. She's relieved to know I'm okay. I don't tell her what happened. It would only worry her. I make up a story and she goes back to sleep.

I lie down on my bed. I stare at the ceiling. I wait for the morning to come. At nine, I shave and put on my suit. I slip the pistol into my waistband and go downstairs. I tell Aunt Norma I have business and need her car.

I park across from the building where the Williamses have their office. I join the people in the lobby and wait for the elevator. We get onboard. I press the button for the tenth floor. Everyone acts as if they're invisible. The doors open. I get out. I chamber a round in the pistol. I put on the safety and stick the gun back in my waistband.

The receptionist looks up as I stride through the door. She smiles and asks if I have an appointment. I blow past her. I say nothing. I ignore her calling after me. Voices come from the other side of Garland's door. I open it and find both brothers inside. I reach for my gun. Garland rises from his chair; he looks at the pistol in my hand and smiles.

"Did you come here to kill me?" Garland says.

I stand in the doorway. I look at the pistol. I turn my wrist so I can see the gun from different angles. The blue-black metal reflects the light. Its weight feels good in my hand. The gun is the perfect tool.

Garland takes a step toward me. He laughs and says, "Killing me? That'd take guts. Not sure you have any, but it'd take some all the same."

I move my gaze from the gun to Garland, from Garland to his brother. Their eyes show the contempt they have for me. My arm grows heavy. I can barely hold the pistol. To aim it would take more than I have.

Garland takes another step and says, "Suppose I loan you some of my guts? Will that bring your friends back? That is, if you shoot me? Would that help you, Tommy, if I loaned you some guts?"

Edward gets up. He walks past his brother and says, "You may have the idea, but you haven't thought it through. There's a difference between having an idea and executing it. Like finding a missing girl, not just looking for her. Or getting through a recording session without throwing up."

The gun remains in my hand, but it points to the floor.

"What did you think I would do," Edward says, "when you stuck your nose where it doesn't belong?"

As Edward walks up beside me, the hair on my neck rises. I can't tell what's causing it. Then I see it. His tie tack, it matches the cufflinks June gave me. And it confirms that Dale never had anything to do with it.

I put the gun in my pocket and pull out the silk bag. I open it and let the cufflinks roll into my hand. I pick one up and hold it out and say, "I have your cufflinks, Edward."

"They're a handsome set, but they're not mine."

I look at Garland, then back at Edward.

"Cut the kidding. They're a perfect match with the tie tack you have on. Helen took these. They belonged to the man she'd been seeing."

"I have no idea what you're talking about," he says.

I step forward till I am inches from his face.

"Stop lying, Edward. It was you all along. It was you. You sent Helen away to have your baby with the understanding it would be put up for adoption. And everyone thought her running away was just another one of Helen's tantrums. You thought you had it all planned. That's why you wanted some other detective to do the job, one who would do whatever you asked. But I started poking my nose around. And that's when you decided Helen needed to come clean."

I stick my finger into Edward's chest.

"But not completely clean. You had Dale Martins. He was the perfect fall guy. No one suspected you. And it wasn't hard to get your brother's wife to believe such a story. And whether you planned it or not, Mrs. Williams did you a…"

"Damn you, Edward!" Garland shouts. I turn around. Garland points a revolver at his brother. I drop the cufflinks and reach for the gun in my pocket.

"Hold still, Tommy!" Garland shouts as he aims the gun back and forth between me and his brother. He takes a step forward, holding the revolver in his big hand and says, "Take that gun out real slow. Use two fingers, and drop it on the floor."

I do what he says. Edward holds still.

"Kick it here."

I kick the gun. It slides and stops at Garland's feet. He picks it up with his free hand and sets it on the desk.

"Garland," I say. "What are you going to do now? Are you going to kill your brother?"

Garland laughs, "I told you I won't forgive whoever's responsible."

"And that makes you a better father? Does that make you a man? That's just your vanity. It has nothing to do with Helen."

He takes another step closer toward Edward and me. His long arm extends; the gun barrel looks like a window into death.

"Your brother may be less than swine and he deserves punishment, but is it for you to decide?"

Garland points the gun at his brother's chest. Edward groans.

"Garland, you can't play out some Cain and Abel story here. You kill your brother and they'll fry you. You're not going to wander the Earth with a mark on your head."

Garland thumbs back the hammer on the revolver. I hear the cylinder rotate.

"You shoot your brother and you're done," I tell him.

The room stinks. I turn my head. Edward stands next to me. I see a dark stain come through his pants. Garland makes a noise like a growl. His eyes look small, his face shows no expression. The gun in his big hand shakes.

A flash. I feel nothing. Then I feel nothing but pain as my belly absorbs the lead. The bullet careens inside me. It shatters bone and ruptures tissue, then exits below my ribcage. I fall to the floor. My body feels cold, and what little air I can get into my lungs begins to mix with blood.

Garland drops the revolver. He puts a hand over his face. He staggers back. Everything goes quiet. The only word I can get out is, "Evelyn."

EPILOGUE

IT LOOKS LIKE snow. My eyes readjust. I'm sprawled out in a cotton field and my belly hurts so bad. I feel like it's been blown apart and that my vitals are hanging outside my body. I look at my hand; it's covered in blood.

My bloodstained hand reminds me of when I was five or six. I'd run smack into a window of a storm door and I cut the palm of that very same hand. I remember my momma used a cotton ball to wipe away the blood. She hums as she uses a pair of tweezers to pull shards of windowpane out of my skin. And all the while, I sit safely on my daddy's lap. My parents love me and my tears stop flowing. I had forgotten about that, but in the cotton field it all came back and it made me feel that I would be okay.

Lying on my back, I move my hand down to my belly. It takes all the energy I have, as if I'd spent an entire lifetime picking cotton in that field. I try to look up. My heavy head falls backward twice and, on the third time, to the ground.

My eyes reopen. I'm still in the field. Hours have passed, and the sun is now a blistering red ball of fire low in the sky. A fetid wind blows, covering me with dust that sticks to my bloodstained clothes. My belly burns as either bile or stomach acid leaks within me. My throat cries out in thirst. Dry blood crusts and cracks in scales upon my hands. I feel something tickling, and I look to see a column of ants crawling over me.

A crow caws and the noise of its wings breaks my

thoughts. A shadow touches upon my face. I look up to see a silhouette of a man walking toward me. He's too far away and his face too in shadow for me to identify him. All I can do is wait.

That figure of a man trudges on without a sound like some soldier on a mission that cannot be contravened. It seems to come three steps forward, then two steps back. Never quite reaching me, yet the figure is implacable. It moves forward. It comes for me where I lie. The sand grows sticky and black with my blood. Finally, the man gets near. He stands above me and looks down.

"Whatcha doin' here, Tommy?"

"I got shot. They must've dumped me."

Dan sets down the sack he keeps his guitar in and sits next to me.

"That's a hell of a thing. What they shoot you fo?"

"Putting my nose into other people's business."

"Well you was always curious. The guitar? You keep up with it?"

I try to smile and cough up a ball of blood.

"Yeah, I did. I never thanked you for teaching me."

Dan removes a handkerchief from his pocket, and he wipes away the blood from my mouth and chin and the sweat from around my eyes.

"You never forgot me, Tommy. That's a thank you in it of itself."

I hold out my hand to Dan, and he takes it and holds it firm. His hand feels warm, and I realize I've been shivering. Dan closes his eyes and hums a tune that sounds like one he played for me so many years ago.

"Tommy, you know somethin'. When you was a kid, I never got to say a proper goodbye."

The memory of that afternoon causes my throat to tighten.

"Do you know what your daddy told me? That time he caught me teaching you guitar."

"No, I watched from the window."

Dan's smiles as tears roll down his cheeks.

"He told me how much he loved you. And how hard it was for him after he came back from the war and all. Hard for him to get to know you again. He saw the way you and I was. He saw it was more than just teaching you guitar."

Dan looks at my belly.

"Your daddy may have been a war hero, but he was afraid he done lost you to me. Yeah. So he asked me to go away. Not come back again, and to leave the two of you alone. Now what kind of man would I be to stand between a man and his son?"

The tightness in my throat is replaced with another kind of ache, and I think about the pain my daddy felt. Not just the pain from the shrapnel that riddled his shoulder and chest, or the pain from his leg blown off from a grenade. But the pain of seeing friends die. And the pain of coming home not a whole of a man. And the pain of working a tedious job in which the only satisfaction he received came from making sure his sister and I lived comfortably.

And along with all that came the pain from his inability to return to being the father he once had been. And how in his final days, with the cancer growing in his lungs, I was stationed overseas and not there to say goodbye. Or to make his last moments comfortable. Or to know what he was thinking.

Dan lets go of my hand as he says, "I gots to be headin' on."

"You have to leave so soon?" I ask.

Dan picks up his sack and holds it under his arm. He

looks to the sky to measure the time by the angle of the sun as it rolls west.

"I gots my own life to live. And you gots yours. But neither I nor your daddy's really gone as long as you remember us by. And you know somethin'? You ain't either if I remember you."

Dan sets the sack over his shoulder and walks between two rows of cotton. His silhouette is rimmed scorching red by the setting sun. And as he walks he sings:

"My head's on fire, momma
  Feels like it's burnin' one hunred and three
  Oh, my head's on fire, momma
  Feels like it's burnin' one hunred and three
  If that fever don't break soon
  That's gonna be the end o' me.

"Doctor swears he's comin'
  Just as fast as he can
  Oooh, doctor swears he's comin'
  Just as fast as he can
  But if he don't git here soon
  Y'all wave bye bye to Dan.

"Oh, if that fever don't quit
  Call me a cabinet maker soon
  If that fever don't up and quit
  Call the cabinet maker soon
  'Cuz I won't need no doctor
  I'll need a casket by tomorrow noon.

"My brain's on fire, momma
  Feels like it's burnin' one hunred and four
  My poor brain's on fire, momma

Feels like it's burnin' one hunred and four
Oh, if my fever don't break soon
Ol' Dan won't be around no more."

"We had to replace nearly half his blood. Continue with the antibiotics. And let me know when his fever breaks."

"I'll let you know, Dr. Manker."

I open my eyes. I'm in bed. A doctor and nurse are speaking at the door. Next to the bed, I see Evelyn asleep in a chair. Her chestnut brown hair glows in a beam of sunlight. I watch her eyelids flutter in her sleep, and I see her chest rise and fall. Her lips are slightly parted. I smile and whisper hello to the freckles around her eyes and nose. I wait for her to wake up. And when she does, I know exactly what I'll do.

ABOUT THE AUTHOR

 Robert R. Moss was a member of the Washington, D.C. music scene in the early 1980s. He played bass in several bands, most notably Artificial Peace and Government Issue. His music was released on Dischord Records and other labels, and, as in the early days of Sun Records, it was a time when new things were happening in rock 'n' roll. During those few exciting years, Robert played on the bill with numerous bands including the Bad Brains, Minor Threat, S.O.A., Black Flag and Channel 3. Venues where he performed include CBGBs, the Peppermint Lounge, A7, the Wilson Center, Oscar's Eye, the Mabuhay Gardens and many more across the United States.

Now, more than 30 years later and with the benefit of hindsight, Robert draws on his experiences—along with the accounts of others and his imagination—and places them into a work of fiction set years before he was born. In what is his first novel, Robert tells a detective/coming-of-age-story that goes beyond music and crime and speaks to issues of race, as well as to universal ideas of becoming an adult in a world that centers on youth.

Robert has worked in the film, television and advertising industries and currently lives in Portland, Oregon, with his wife and son.